DEATH RITE

A mound of summer flowers covered Pete's grave. Robin looked back at it and shivered. She hadn't known Pete all that well but the picture of him riding his motorbike with such energy stayed in her mind vividly. And now ... just a slip of a foot, just a moment of bad judgement and he was gone, wiped out.

Once again she wondered what on earth he had been doing at the old quarry. What had made him fall? The police had come, of course. Questions had been asked. An accident, obviously. What else? Pete had no enemies. The thought of anyone pushing him was just unthinkable. But ... what had he been doing there? No one seemed to know.

Look out for:

Lawless & Tilley: The Secrets of the Dead
Lawless & Tilley: Deep Waters
Malcolm Rose

The Beat: Sudden Death
David Belbin

Publish or Die!
Alan Durant

POINT CRIME

DEAD RITE

Jill Bennett

SCHOLASTIC

Scholastic Children's Books
Commonwealth House, 1–19 New Oxford Street,
London WC1A 1NU, UK
a division of Scholastic Ltd
London ~ New York ~ Toronto ~ Sydney ~ Auckland

First published in the UK by Scholastic Ltd, 1997

Copyright © Jill Bennett, 1997

ISBN 0 590 13935 5

Typeset by TW Typesetting, Midsomer Norton, Somerset
Printed by Cox & Wyman Ltd, Reading, Berks.

10 9 8 7 6 5 4 3 2 1

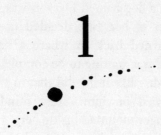

1

"**D**on't do that!"

Robin spun round to see where the command had come from. A young man stood looking at her from the gap between two young sycamore trees. He was frowning.

Robin didn't reply at once. She glowered in his direction, trying to think of something suitably cutting to make him wish he had never opened his mouth. If she wanted to spray crimson circles on the trunks of trees, she would do so. She shook the can of spray paint defiantly. A brown dog burst through some brambles and ran towards her, barking.

"Darwin, heel!" the young man commanded again, stopping the dog in its tracks.

"Darwin!" Robin poured all the scorn she was capable of into the name. Only someone who obviously thought he was better than most would give a name like that to his dog. The young man wore his hair long and waving around his face, and she could see he had a leather thong with coloured beads round his neck. Someone who looked like a wayside poet and had a dog named Darwin was not going to get the better of her. She decided to say nothing more and turned back to where a half circle of crimson paint was waiting to be completed.

"You wouldn't like it if I did that to you."

Robin turned on him. "Just mind your own business!" Anger mounted inside her.

"It *is* my business, it's everyone's business. The trees can't defend themselves." The young man's voice stayed maddeningly calm, his face stern.

"It is obvious," Robin said icily, "that you wouldn't recognize a work of art if it came towards you in a clown costume! I'm not hurting the trees, I'm adding to them. These circles are the heart's blood of every tree, they stand for the joy they give to others and the life they enhance. Enhance!" She shouted the word at the still figure. "Absolute morons like you wouldn't know the meaning of the word. Like most of the people in this godforsaken village!"

She dropped the can of paint into the bag lying on the ground beside her with a gesture of disgust, zipped it up viciously, and marched away. She was seething.

Robin's rage turned against the village. She felt, she thought wryly, like some uprooted tree must feel when it has been replanted into alien soil and climate.

As she walked to the edge of the wood with long, frustrated strides, she cursed the day her parents were left a small nursery garden on the edge of the village of Godmore.

It was the beginning of August now, and ever since February, when her family had moved here, she had felt as if she would curl up and die if she couldn't get back to the city.

She couldn't blame them for coming, she knew that, and she didn't. Her father was a gardener by nature and profession; he had tended the council parks near their London flat for years. So it was a heaven-sent miracle when her mother's brother left her his nursery garden and cottage in Godmore. It had wiped out their mortgage problems and un-certain future at one swipe.

But ... oh, how she longed for their former life! She even longed for her old school where she had planned her future as an artist, a sculptor. That's where her heart lay. Now she had to join a sixth-form college in a local market town and do her A-levels. A-levels! When she wanted to get going so badly! Robin kicked a stone by the side of the lane and watched it skitter over the rough tarmac.

A motorbike came round the bend in front of her far too fast. The rider and passenger were leaning into the bend as they roared round it. Robin, squashed into the hedge, stung her hand on some nettles and looked after its retreating exhaust.

Pete, she thought. Had to be, it was his bike – and

3

was that Judith on the back? The hank of roughly plaited hair hanging down from under the helmet looked like hers. No one else she knew had hair that red. Robin had only seen her at a distance, but the colour stood out a mile. She sucked at her stung hand thoughtfully.

So Judith had arrived in Godmore again. That meant that Richard, her brother, was here too. This did not help Robin's black mood one jot. Judith and Richard Longstaff had been spending holidays at Godmore for years. Their parents, both journalists, had an old farmhouse there, and the family retreated to it from the chaos of London when they could. As they came for their longest time in the summer, they were sometimes referred to as the Godmore Swallows.

Robin had glimpsed them earlier that Easter. She bitterly envied them the good fortune that gave them London to live in. She'd never come to this forgotten hole, ever.

But what was Judith up to, riding pillion on Pete's bike? He was going out with Allison, everybody knew that. They had been seen together, arms entwined, obviously an item. Robin gave a mirthless snort. If that was so, this would probably put the cat among the pigeons. She welcomed the thought that it might cause disruption amongst the small group of village teenagers. Anything to shake the place up a bit.

She and Anna had been told a lot about the Londoners. The villagers became slightly defensive whenever they were mentioned, which was intriguing.

Certainly they brought a city glamour with them, and this both attracted and threatened their contemporaries. They were inclined to feel inferior to this highly educated pair who seemed to look down on them from the lofty heights of superior knowledge.

Wasn't Pete a bit out of his depth with Judith?

Robin shrugged. It was nothing to do with her. They were all boring anyway.

She arrived at the small wooden gate that led into her garden and tugged it open. Trying not to read the name, Greensleeves, printed in capitals on a board in the middle of the top bar, she walked up the short, concrete path. The name was another thorn in her already punctured side. It spoke of all the cottagey tweeness she hated.

She had said, right at the start, that No. 2 The Cottages had a bit more dignity about it, but her mother had just smiled and said she rather liked the name. It made her think of old-fashioned roses and stately dances.

No use Robin telling her that green was the colour that Tudor ladies of the town wore, as a badge of recognition, on their sleeves; her mother just laughed and said she didn't know where Robin got her ideas. She wouldn't mind if it was changed to Green Fingers, though, she had added; that would suit them.

Green Fingers! Robin thought of that now and snorted with disgust as she skirted the side wall of the cottage and headed for the back door. It was hot and she was thirsty.

Behind the cottage, the nursery garden stretched away. It was a sensible size, with room to propagate as well as sell plants. Mr Robson's brother-in-law had cultivated and sold a great deal of young herbaceous and annual plants to local garden centres. The rest he put to vegetables. Mr Robson hoped to do the same. But the plants that he wanted to rear were not vegetables, he had no feeling for those, he said. He was going to specialize in some of the flowers he grew in London parks, flowers he knew about. Every sort of pelargonium for one, and fuchsias and ... all the spring bulbs... His eyes grew misty as he planned.

Robin sometimes wished she could enter his world of planting out, compost and seed propagation, but it was another planet to her, she could never walk about on it. Not the way Anna could. Anna, her twin, who was like her in almost every way but this.

"Hi, Robin!"

Anna came out of the nearest poly tunnel and waved. "Put the kettle on, I'm dying, it's so hot in there! Dad's at his last gasp too." Her long, fair hair, tied into a ponytail that morning, was sticking to her back and dark strands had escaped to fall against her face. She pushed them away.

Robin slung her bag on to the kitchen table and turned on the tap. Automatically, she switched on the radio with the same gesture she used to switch on the kettle. Radio One filled the small room, which was warmer than outside, if that were possible.

Anna's figure blocked the light as she stood in the

doorway to tap the earth from her gloves and leave them outside along with her boots.

"The Longstaffs are back," Robin said shortly.

"Oh? Seen them?" Anna's feet left sweaty imprints across the vinyl floor as she padded over to fetch the teapot.

"Saw Judith – on Pete's bike."

"Pete's?"

"Yeah, surprised me too." Robin put tea bags into the pot and gave it a stir. "And there's a strange man in Holly Wood."

"Strange?"

"Well, I haven't seen him before. He has a dog."

"What kind?"

"I don't know. For goodness' sake, Anna!" Robin spoke testily. She could take or leave dogs.

"I saw Deb in the shop this morning," Anna said. "She says there are travellers in the bridleway by the wood. They have an old van, could be him." Anna poured tea into thick china mugs, bright with flowers on their sides.

"I'll take Dad's. Mum's gone into town." She ignored her boots and walked carefully, barefoot, towards the poly tent where the shadow of her father's figure could be seen moving behind the plastic.

The afternoon news began on the radio.

Robin took her tea and sat outside on a bench against the kitchen wall. She was dressed in an old black T-shirt that she had chopped off just above her waistline and she flapped its ragged edge, trying to create a draught. Even her tattered jeans, torn at the knees, were clinging to her.

Anna came back and sat beside her.

Side by side, the similarity between the two girls was much more obvious than at first glance. Just seventeen, both about average height, slender and well-formed, with the same ways of walking and speaking, their twinship was easily discernible. But although the conformation of their oval faces was the same, and the colour of their fair skin, the difference in their personalities had begun to leave its mark.

Anna was like her father: creative and good natured to the brink of being placid. She, too, loved to grow things, content to await the turning of the seasons. Her eyes were calm and accepting above an untroubled mouth, which was always ready to smile. She tended to wear soft shades. Long T-shirts that had been dyed with colours that merged and blended, worn over faded cotton trousers and some-times over long, patterned skirts.

Robin, the rebel, restless and seeking, was impatient with people who didn't think the way she did. Wearing black mainly, with jeans always, never a skirt if she could help it, she was creative like Anna but not in the same way. She had sudden ideas that had to be carried out instantly. Not for her the waiting for nature to take its course. If something was planted one day, it was no good unless it was fully grown by the next. She was suffocating in the village. Also like Anna, her hair fell over her shoulders to be bound with a loose, untidy piece of cord. Her blue eyes were alert and sparkled when she got excited and her mouth was often set in a challenging line.

Unconsciously, the sisters grasped their mugs of tea in both hands, reflecting one another's gesture.

Anna tensed. She put a hand on Robin's knee.

"Listen."

"Reports have been coming in," the newscaster's even voice floated out from the kitchen, "of more incidents of animal mutilation on several farms in the area…"

"What area?"

"Shush, Rob."

"A farmer in Porlon reported that three of his cows had been cut around their udders. This makes it the fourth report of this kind in the last fortnight. All the farms affected have been in the area around the market town of Farrow. The police are making detailed inquiries, but the farmers say they will be setting their own watch until the person or persons responsible for this outrage is caught."

The girls looked at each other.

"Porlon is just over the hill." Anna's gentle face looked worried.

"Rotten cowards!" Robin scowled; she couldn't stand cruelty in any form. Then she added under her breath. "Must be some nutter driven to insanity by this godawful place."

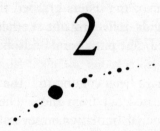

2

Looking at herself in the mirror of the hairdressing salon, Robin grinned at what she saw.

"Thanks," she said to the stylist who was fluttering around behind her. "It's great."

"Well." The stylist was trying to be non-committal. "You could say it's different."

Robin surveyed herself from a different angle.

"Great job," she said and she rose, preparing to pay.

The stylist took a quick look at her own image in the glass, as if to reassure herself that she, at least, still maintained the standards required by her usual clientele. Satisfied, she beckoned to the junior to sweep up the long strands of Robin's fair, straight hair lying on the salon floor. The junior did this, stealing furtive glances at Robin's shorn head in the mirror.

Still grinning, Robin swung out of the glass door

and on to the main street, leaving the stylist free to raise her eyes to heaven and the two other clients, seated in various stages of blow-dry and trims, to put down their magazines.

"Well," the stylist exploded. "She knew what she wanted, all right – even brought the colour with her – didn't think we'd have it here. She was dead right."

The crumpled remains of Cobalt Blue Clearwater Colourant still lay on her working tray and she swept it into the bin.

"All that lovely hair," mourned one of the ladies.

"Half an inch all over," said the stylist with a sniff, "not a millimetre longer." She allowed her outrage to show.

"You didn't half use a lot of gel on it." There was a touch of admiration in the junior's voice. "Stood up like she'd had a fright." She giggled.

"Get on, Tracy. Mrs Thomas is waiting."

Mrs Thomas, a thin woman with her hair swathed in a towel, looked stunned. "I just couldn't believe it when you started to take the clippers to it. All that pink scalp above her ears. Whatever do you think she thought she looked like?"

"Comes from London," said the stylist, as if that explained everything. "Now, dear, how do *you* want it today?"

Hairdressing, as practised in the best salon on the main street of Farrow, settled down and the ladies of Farrow relaxed back in their chairs. Hot air, roaring around their ears inside their hair dryers, successfully cut them off from the world and any troubling thoughts.

Robin, deeply satisfied with her changed appearance, and catching covert glimpses of herself in shop windows, made her way to the bus station for the only afternoon bus back to Godmore.

The village sported one shop and one public house. The shop was run by Bob Merton, and the pub was called The Staff and Pilgrim.

There was a bus that ran through the village twice a week, on Tuesdays and Fridays. It picked up passengers at ten in the morning and brought them home again on the five o'clock from Farrow. A local railway branch line ran a few trains to the nearest large junction, but if people really wanted to get about from Godmore, they needed wheels to do so.

The children of the village were bussed to local schools as the village school was long closed and now a desirable family home. Most of the children went to the comprehensive school in Farrow, except for a few wealthier ones, whose parents sent them to private schools in the district, of which there were several. These children were mainly carried by car to school, whilst the others, when big enough, biked and later bought mopeds. They all valued, and longed for, the independence that their own transport could bring them.

This Friday evening was sultry and heavy. Clouds had gathered during the long summer day, but had not loosed any rain to bring relief from the sticky heat. Some younger children were circling the village on their bikes, running races through the shallow ford made by a small stream that wound its way through Godmore. It was a finger of the river Far, named the Farling, but the young villagers referred to it as the Gone. An in-joke that only the privileged few would understand.

A small stone bridge spanned the stream where the road through Godmore crossed it. This was at a central point of the village and was a natural meeting place.

Anna was there, sitting on the low wall in a loose pink dress that came to her ankles. Her hair was still wet from washing it after her day in the nursery garden. Greg stood beside her. He was the only son of a local farmer. Sun-tanned and muscular, seeming almost to burst the buttons on his blue shirt, he was shy of manner. Anna looked ethereal beside him. He said little, but he was never very far away from her side.

Deb, Pete's plump younger sister, sat on the wall on the other side of the narrow road. Occasionally a car would slow down and glide between them, but it never interrupted their conversation for long.

Deb said, "He's ever so late. D'you think he's coming?"

"Thomas is always late," Greg shrugged.

There was a noise of a motorbike revving up after the last bend. It burst upon the bridge and braked.

Pete stood, straddling it.

"Thomas not here yet?"

"No." His sister spoke meaningfully and looked at him with a grimace. "But someone else is coming." She turned her head and stared up the road. Everyone else turned and stared in the same direction.

"Longstaffs are here again – must be summer!" Deb added without enthusiasm.

Anna watched as the two Longstaffs, Judith and Richard, approached. She was interested in them. She had to admit they seemed exotic creatures of sophistication, having journalists for parents. Not any old journalists, but news hounds for national papers. She stole a glance at Pete's face. After Robin had told her about seeing Judith on his bike, she wondered how he felt about her.

Pete threw a pebble into the stream and watched the ripples intently.

"Greetings all." Judith waved her hand airily. "What's new?"

Silence fell. There didn't seem any answer to that. Nothing much was new in Godmore.

Richard, a step or two behind his sister, broke it.

"Hello," he spoke cheerfully, but with a slight diffidence. "It's us again."

His greeting had more success than Judith's. The little group shifted and relaxed.

"Evenin'." Greg tried to sound casual, as if the Longstaffs were always there. He didn't mind Richard, but Judith, with her airs and graces, really got up his nose.

Judith marched over to Pete and stood against the wall beside him. She looked up into his face, as if he was the only one there. She smiled at him.

"Hi, Pete."

Pete straightened up and smiled back. He had been wondering if she would single him out again after their bike ride. You never knew with her. She could be hot one minute and cold the next. He had never expected her to agree to ride with him in the first place. She had never looked at him before.

Anna, watching quietly, thought, Pete's blushing. She sensed his confusion. It wasn't just the warmth of the evening that was making his face bright pink.

Deb noticed too. A spurt of anger against these two familiar outsiders jabbed at her. She was good friends with Allison, and Judith was spoiling everything, as usual.

When they arrived in the village everything got difficult somehow. It was hard to put a finger on it, but it happened every time. It had not always been like that. When they were younger they had tried to be part of the group. But now Judith had turned eighteen, was poised to go to university. She was obviously bright with a bright future ahead. It would be a far brighter future that any one of them might hope of having. Deb's mum and dad had never lived anywhere else than Godmore, and Deb did not expect to move far. Envy and suspicion had created a distance between them now.

"Staying long?" Deb directed that, with an edge it wasn't difficult to hear, straight at Judith.

Judith picked it up and turned it back. She leaned against Pete's bike.

"As long as we can stand it."

Deb's eyes remained on Judith's face; she was not deflected. Her voice's edge became a cutting blade. "Where's Allison this evening, Pete?" she asked him. "Isn't she coming?"

Anna felt surprise. This wasn't like little Deb. She was the youngest of the group and seemed content just to tag along with everyone. But there were hidden depths to her, obviously. Loyalty to Pete and Allison had goaded her to challenge Judith of all people. Battle lines had been drawn and, Anna knew, Deb was no match for Judith.

Judith turned slowly and looked at Pete. She raised an eyebrow as if waiting for him to say something.

Pete's mouth opened obediently, but nothing came out.

Judith's lip lifted in a slight sneer. She turned back to Deb.

"She's probably at home, looking in her crystal ball, weighing up her chances," she said lightly and with complete assurance. Deb's gaze faltered and fell before Judith's clear gaze. She roughly pulled a long grass from its socket and chewed at it. Her eyes had begun to water and her round cheeks flushed red.

As silence fell heavily, Anna got off the wall. Enough's enough, she thought.

"Hello, I'm Anna," she said to Judith. "We haven't met. How do you do?"

Greg looked at her with admiration. She sounded cool and in control and on the same ground with Judith. He liked her London voice and the way her words came over, light and clipped. His own West Country tones were warm and rounded in comparison.

"Judith," said Judith, looking her over. "This here's my brother, Richard." Judith's voice had a deliberate drawl. She indicated Richard with a jerk of her thumb, not looking at him. Anna glanced in his direction and saw that he seemed to be quite unruffled by the recent tense atmosphere.

"Hi," he said and smiled at her.

His hair was as red as his sister,'s, but his blue eyes gave nothing away. Where does he fit in? Anna wondered. He's in Judith's shadow, that's for sure.

"Well, well. The Godmore swallows are here again!"

Everyone started. Thomas had arrived and nobody had heard him approach. He was carrying a bulging plastic bag.

"You're late," said Greg, glad to see him.

"Let battle commence." Thomas rattled his plastic bag.

"Unwise!" Pete exclaimed, relieved to be let off the hook and laughing a bit too loudly. "The cans'll go pop."

Thomas was eighteen. He could buy beer and

hand it round as long as it was not in a pub or shop. He had been the leader of the group for years. For one thing he was the tallest, being six feet and very rangy. His job in Farrow, in the cheese factory, had allowed him to adopt a world-weary, know-it-all air. He had been very popular when they were all young, they were happy for him to take the lead then. Now they continued in the same old pattern, but outwardly only. They knew him too well. They knew he bent the law wherever he could, thinking it clever.

He liked to boast about his latest exploits with his workmates, who flattered him with their rounds of beer and slaps on the back but didn't really like him.

His old friends accepted him for what he was, habit and loyalty playing their part. They also enjoyed the occasional perks that his buccaneering brought in. One Christmas all of them, and a few older citizens as well, had demolished a case of ginger wine he had "found". Godmore would always remember that Christmas!

They didn't ask him where he found it, or his flashy watches and different leather jackets. But they ceased to trust him with their old confidences as they used to do. They knew he wouldn't think twice about betraying them, if it served his need. Honesty and Thomas had become uneasy bedfellows.

He handed round the cans. The girls had Coke, he opened a can of lager and held one out to Pete.

Pete looked at Judith. "Want some?"

Judith shrugged scornfully. "Warm beer? Not my

tipple, thank you." She turned away.

Pete didn't want to lose her interest, not after he was getting on so well with her, or so he thought.

"You're right. Come on, what say we take off for town?" He slapped the saddle on his motorbike and hoped he sounded exciting and unrefusable. Then, in a rush, he added, "I got a job."

Everyone stared at him. Pete had been trying to find work since he left school.

"You never said." Deb felt hurt. Why'd he have to tell that Judith before her? She was family, after all. "What is it?" She was really very glad for him.

Pete managed to look both proud and sheepish at once.

"I'll tell you at the pub." This still to Judith.

Judith hesitated, then she turned round to him.

"OK. But I'll drive my car. You can park your bike at the cottage. Coming, Richard?"

Pete felt the wind being taken out of his sails. Judith was giving a series of commands. She had her mother's Golf for the summer and suddenly his big moment of importance and his beloved motorbike shrank to nothing beside that. Disconcerted, he let off the brake and prepared to drop in behind her.

"Actually," Richard said pleasantly, "I have things I want to do on the computer. You two go."

"Pete!" Deb implored him. "Tell me!"

"Save your breath, Deb," Thomas said. "He's made it up. There isn't a job, he's just said that to impress *her*." His eyes lingered on Judith's retreating

19

back. Her plait of fiery hair swinging a little. His expression was hooded and difficult to read. Then suddenly he caught sight of a figure walking down the hill towards them and he turned.

"Holeee cow!" he exclaimed, in an exaggerated Western accent. "Just look what the cat dragged in!"

Robin had walked round the curve in the road and was almost upon them.

Silence greeted her as everyone stared in her direction. Judith stopped in her tracks and turned round to look. Electric blue spikes of hair stuck up all over her scalp, some of which was neatly exposed in two swathes, cut from forehead to nape, over both ears. These were pierced, as Anna's were, but now her gold studs were plainly visible. She reminded Richard of some daring pirate, facing them all as they stared at her. Robin grinned back at them.

"Hello all," she said, standing in the middle of the road, with her hands in her jeans' pockets and her legs planted firmly apart.

Anna took a step towards her sister and looked into her face. After a moment, while Robin returned her look, she smiled.

"What on earth did they say?" she asked her.

"Mother hit the roof, Dad walked out," Robin replied, understanding her. "Like it?"

Anna said nothing, but continued to smile at Robin, and it seemed to the group watching that the two girls were carrying on a dialogue that only they could hear. In spite of the different way they now looked from one another, their close similarity was still apparent.

"Well, well." Judith strolled forward. "Ms London meets the Worzels." She spoke deliberately in banner headlines. She knew she was being rude but just couldn't resist it. Robin was stealing her thunder.

Robin turned her head to stare at her, breaking her silent bond with Anna. Judith's sudden attack surprised her. She didn't even know her. What on earth was her problem?

Anna swung round on Judith. She wasn't going to allow her to vent her sarcasm on Robin.

"Practising to be cub reporter on the *Godmore Echo*?" she asked mildly, her eyes cold.

Judith shrugged.

"Come on, if you're coming," she flung at Pete and turned on her heel.

"Bye." Pete followed her, pushing his bike, looking as if he wished he could think of something to say. Richard, still unruffled, waved a hand and followed them.

Greg's eyes strayed back to Anna, relieved she was not the type to change her looks so radically like her twin.

Deb wondered if her parents knew about Pete's job and now wished she was at home in front of the telly. She broke open her can of Coke and took a fizzy gulp. The evening was not turning out very well.

Thomas rumpled her short brown hair with a careless hand and opened his can of lager with a swagger. He was trying to think of something clever to say about Robin's new look.

Robin said, "I thought Pete was Allison's boyfriend."

Deb gave a snort. "Judith just looked at him and he fell over. That's Her Majesty for you."

"Do you fancy Pete, then?" Thomas asked Robin with the suspicion of a leer. "Did you get your hair done specially?" He stepped closer to where Robin stood in the road. She didn't give way.

"You foreigners are all the same." She recognized this as heavy banter. "You think we country bumpkins don't know a trick or two."

He towered over Robin, and still she stayed where she was. He had a lean, craggy face and a slick of dark hair that fell over his forehead. His eyes were very dark brown and deeply set in their sockets.

Robin sensed that her new looks had worked like a kind of challenge to Thomas. She was of interest to him now, whereas before he had barely noticed her. Perhaps she would act like a sort of trophy if she went out with him. She had heard stories about him from the others but at the moment she didn't care. Thomas offered her the prospect of some excitement, even danger, and the way she was now, danger had an attractive feel about it. Anyway, she liked his dark looks and the powerful motorbike he rode.

She put out her hand for his can of beer. He gave it to her and she held his eyes as she took a gulp. Thomas gave a short laugh and went to snatch it back. Swiftly, Robin threw it in the stream beneath the bridge.

"Gone," she said, with a glint in her eyes.

Deb laughed. She was glad that Thomas had been bettered.

Thomas swore.

Anna sighed. "For goodness' sake," was all she said and prepared to clamber down to the stream to retrieve the can.

At that moment a girl on a bicycle shot around the bend and came to an abrupt halt on the bridge. She was hot and panting a little.

"Greg! I've been looking all over!" There was high drama in her voice. "There's something *weird* going on at the farm!"

"Hi, Allison," Greg said calmly. "What d'you mean, *weird*?"

He didn't stir. Everyone knew Allison's love of dramatic situations.

Allison Parker looked irritated with him. Really, she thought, the world could come to an end, black paint could fall from the sky and Greg would just shrug his shoulders.

"I thought," she said, a little heavily, "you would be interested to know that a police car just drove into your yard as I passed the gate."

"Yeah?" Greg straightened up. "What did they want?"

"Well, I don't know, do I?" She was slightly mollified by his show of interest. "But I'm sure you ought to go and find out. Perhaps –" a new thought struck her – "the infamous cow-cutter has struck again."

Deb gasped. Gratified, Allison looked around at the now silent group. Thomas sniggered.

"That's not funny." Greg rounded on him. His father's dairy herd was big and prosperous and he was very proud of it. The thought of the dreadful maniac cutting one of their herd was monstrous. Cutting anybody's herd, come to that.

"Better go," he said, turning to Anna. "Could be that PC Plod has just looked in for a chat about neighbourhood watch, but…"

"Go," Anna urged him, hearing the underlying anxiety in his voice.

He set off towards his farm at a brisk trot.

Allison looked around. "Where's Pete?"

There was silence. Thomas opened his mouth to say something, but he caught Deb's eye and, for once, closed it again. To their relief, Allison's interest was somewhere else.

"Oh, I'll catch him later." She mounted her bike and began to pedal furiously, her black hair flapping behind her in several untidy plaits. Born with mousy brown hair, she dyed it jet black to fit the image she had of herself, and wanted others to have, too: of someone mysterious, someone who knew the answers to a great many secret things, and who it was dangerous to cross. Judith's crack about her crystal ball was not so short of the mark.

"Bye," she shouted to them over her shoulder. "Greg!" they heard her call as she rounded a bend. "Greg ... wait for me!"

"Miss Nosy wants to be in at the kill," Thomas observed sarcastically. Because she was called Allison Parker, she had been Nosy all her school days. It was a source of great irritation to her that the ones who knew her best did not take her as seriously as she would like. Allison was determined that one day, she would show them all what she could do.

"Wait till she finds out she's been jilted for Judith." He added this with satisfaction.

Deb said with disgust, "You're a pig, you know that, Thomas?" and walked towards her front gate. She and Pete lived in one of a small row of council cottages lying next to the Gone.

Anna regarded Thomas with distaste.

"Home, Robin?" she asked.

Robin said nothing, she looked at Thomas.

"I got my bike up the pub," he said. "Want to see how fast I can go?" This with another, rather suggestive, leer.

Robin shrugged. "Why not?" She turned to Anna. "See you later."

Anna intuitively understood that Robin's need for excitement made her choose Thomas for a companion, but she felt uneasy. She didn't like him. Fingering the little silver locket that always hung around her neck, she watched them walk round the corner to begin the climb up the village hill to the pub.

3

That Sunday, Robin returned to the wood. Sundays were great deserts of inactivity for her. She felt more of a captive than ever on those days when nearly everyone seemed to have a huge amount to eat for lunch, either at home or at the pub, and spent the rest of the day stretched out in front of their televisions.

In the city she had been able to go to exhibitions or meet her like-minded friends in cafés to argue and talk together about the things that interested them all, but here...

Frustrated, and feeling a bit lonely, she left her parents having a well-earned rest after their lunch; left Anna, who was dreamily looking at a magazine on a sunlounger, and headed for the wood.

It was known locally as Holly Wood, as a great

many ancient holly trees grew on its perimeter, but mostly people referred to it as "the wood", and left it at that.

Robin didn't intend to finish her work of painting the heart of the trees on their bark. Her conflict with the strange young man had deadened her creative urge as far as that was concerned. But the very presence of the crowded trees gave her a sense of belonging that nowhere else in the village did. The patterns that the leaves and branches made on each other and on the brambled ground, lit by sunlight, soothed her and took her thoughts into deep, secret places.

Keen to avoid the site of her interrupted artwork and the bridleway, in case Anna's remark about the van was true, Robin turned into the wood through the gate at its easterly edge. The last thing she wanted was to see anyone else there, anyone who would get in the way of her mood. The strange young man and his dog would most certainly do that.

So she climbed slowly along the furthest edge of the wood away from the west side nearest the village, where the stream ran beside the bridleway, and into the wood itself.

The ground rose uphill quite steeply there, giving, as the trees thinned, glimpses of the flat landscape below it. The wood stretched steadily upwards to the brow of a high ridge. She had never been that way before.

It was so quiet. The heat of early afternoon lay

over everything, bright and oppressive. No bird was singing; even the cattle, in the flat fields below her, were sitting down, chewing rhythmically, and lazily swatting at flies with their tails.

Suddenly, a hurtling figure stumbled through the trees, heedless of the brambles tugging at her legs and ankles. Her head was down, and her fists clenched. She almost bumped into Robin before she saw her, and stopped in her tracks. It was Deb. Her mouth was clamped shut, but her eyes were bulging. She stood, frozen, in front of Robin, her set mouth slackening a little as she recognized her.

"Deb!" Startled, that was all Robin could say.

Still Deb was unable to speak.

Robin grasped her shoulders and squeezed.

"Deb. What's the matter, what's happened?"

Deb drew breath.

"Pete." She gasped the word. "Pete's down the quarry!"

"The quarry?" Robin knew there were old stone workings in the wood. She had never seen them. "Has he fallen?"

Deb nodded dumbly, all the colour draining from her face.

"Is he hurt?" Robin urged her as Deb threatened to go silent again. She gave her shoulder another squeeze.

Deb drew in another rasping breath.

"Dead!" she said, and her legs began to shake.

Robin helped her to the ground and propped her

against a tree trunk. She knelt beside her with her mind racing. If Pete was really hurt, they'd need help fast. Deb couldn't mean he was dead. She was just shocked.

"Where is he, Deb?"

Deb merely shook her head. She pointed up the narrow path with a trembling finger, still unable to speak.

Robin made up her mind. She knew Deb was too shocked, she couldn't run for help, her legs wouldn't take her.

"Wait here for me," she told her, more firmly than she felt, for Pete might be in real trouble. She half scrambled, half ran in the direction of Deb's pointing finger.

All at once she was on it. The mouth of the quarry workings fell away abruptly in front of her feet. It was almost completely hidden by a twining mat of weed and roots; a deep hole left in the floor of the wood.

Some attempt, long ago, had been made to protect the edge of the quarry with a fence. But that was broken now and covered with rampant ivy so that it looked like part of the natural flooring of the wood itself. It had suffered years of neglect.

Robin tried to calm her beating heart as she moved closer to the lip of the hole and peered over the edge of the quarry.

After a moment her eyes adjusted to the dim light of the pit. Pete was down there. She could just see his shape, light against the earth.

"Pete!" she shouted.

There was no answering shout.

"Pete. Are you all right?" Robin realized that she was yelling. No sign of life came from Pete's still figure.

Should I go down there? Robin thought desperately. She knelt down by the side of the hole and stretched herself into it, trying to see clearer.

Now she could just distinguish Pete's pale face, and saw that his head was lying at an impossible angle to his body. His eyes were wide open. Robin drew back in horror. Pete's neck was obviously broken.

Stunned, she stumbled back to Deb. She found her sitting where she had left her, sobbing. The frozen shock had given way to grief. Robin put her arms round her and helped her to get up.

"We'll get help, Deb," she said to the weeping girl. She felt suddenly so much older. "We've got to tell someone, and get him home."

She wanted to ask what they had been doing there, what had happened, but she knew Deb was in no state to tell her.

Grasping Deb under her arm, she supported her steps as they both stumbled shakily down the hill towards Godmore.

Oh God, thought Robin. How can we tell his mum?

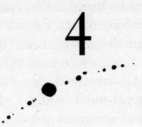

4

The village was stunned by Pete's death.

In its small church, Pete's funeral took place in a downpour of rain. Robin and Anna, standing with their parents, watched his coffin being gently lowered into the wet earth. Tears were pouring down Anna's cheeks, and Robin found that she was noticing little things, like the spouts of rain falling off umbrellas, like a sodden blackbird that was sheltering under the church porch eaves, rather than think of the unbearable lump in her own throat, or look at Deb's white face.

All his friends and most of the village were there. Judith and Richard stood a bit apart. They seemed embarrassed, as if they had no real place there, when the village mourned.

When it was over and the people drifted away, a

few close relations and friends returned to the small house beside the Gone for tea. Robin and Anna were still newcomers to Godmore, so they prepared to go home, after bidding the family goodbye.

A mound of summer flowers covered Pete's grave. Cottage roses and hothouse blooms tangled together in the rain. Robin looked back at it and shivered. She hadn't known Pete all that well, hadn't bothered with him very much, but the picture of him, with Judith behind, riding his motorbike fast and with such energy, stayed in her mind vividly. And now ... just a slip of a foot, just a moment of bad judgement and he was gone, wiped out.

Once again she wondered what on earth he had been doing at the old quarry. What had made him fall? The police had come, of course. Questions had been asked. An accident, obviously. What else? Pete had no enemies. The thought of anyone pushing him was just unthinkable. But ... what had he been doing there? No one, not even Deb, who had found him, seemed to know.

The rain eased and stopped at about six o'clock. A washed, turquoise sky hung limply above the wooded ridge and low fields of Godmore. Cows, eased of their milk, grazed on the fresh grass and chewed reflectively. Greg's dad and elder brother, swishing at nettles with their stout sticks, walked the boundaries of the farm home fields. The cow-cutter, as he was beginning to be called, had to be kept away. They would do this walk in shifts through the night until they were sure the danger was past.

Greg's room at the farm was large and shaded. It was snug in winter and cool in the heat of summer, insulated in both seasons by the thick stone walls. The old farmhouse had low, beamed ceilings and the uneven stone floors were covered with pieces of matting and faded, friendly rugs.

Allison, Thomas, Anna and Robin were already there. Greg said he had asked Judith and Richard, but didn't know if they would come.

Gravely, as if united by a single thought, they all lifted their mugs of farm cider.

Allison said, "To Pete."

"To Pete."

There was a moment's silence.

Thomas stretched out his long legs. He was sitting on an old low sofa covered with a dog blanket.

"If you ask me," he said slowly, "I reckon he was pushed. If I'd been that red-haired bint from London, I'd've done it for a laugh." He looked round the room to see what effect his words might have had.

No one moved. That was just the sort of remark they all expected from Thomas. It was out of place and callous, but they were used to him.

Robin, deliberately ignoring it, asked, "What was he doing up there anyway?"

"Or Deb?" This was Allison. She was dressed in black from head to foot. A heavy jet necklace hung around her neck. Robin guessed she had made her face up with white make-up. She was the picture of the grieving girlfriend.

"Does anyone know what Deb told the police?" Anna stroked the head of Greg's small, rough terrier as she spoke. He was lying against her legs as she sat on the floor, leaning her back against Greg's chair.

No one did.

"If you ask me," Thomas began again, "there's someone who could tell us."

Allison sent him a sharp look.

"No one would be so daft as to ask you," she said.

He returned her look and giggled maliciously. She scowled at him. If Thomas meant her, he was wide of the mark. Her scowl deepened.

The farmhouse front-door bell clattered. It had ceased to ring years ago. Footsteps came up the wooden stairs and along the passage. Judith and Richard came into the room.

"Hello," Richard said. Judith waved her hand at them.

Greg poured them each a mug of cider.

"Cheers," said Judith, looking solemn.

Allison was taken by surprise at the pure hatred she felt for the other girl. She should have had the special place in the group as Pete's sorrowing girl-friend. But now she knew, and so did everybody else, that Judith had taken that place.

"There's one consolation…" She spoke with her brown eyes glittering a little. "If we really want to know what happened to Pete, I can find out." She stared hard at Judith.

"What are you on about, Allison?" Judith stared back at her. She understood Allison's antipathy, and shared it.

Allison allowed the edges of her mouth to smile.

"I mean, there are ways, ways that I know, things that I can do, to get to the bottom of Pete's … accident." The slight pause was deliberate.

Thomas laughed harshly. He was watching Judith closely. "You mean, your mumbo–jumbo, Allison? Give us a break."

Robin was getting fed up with all the bickering.

"Judith," she addressed her directly. "What did you tell the police?"

"Why me?" Judith was hedging. "Look, I didn't come here to be interrogated."

Anna joined in.

"You know why you. You were with Pete on Saturday; Mum and I saw you in Farrow when we went in to make a delivery."

"Saturday isn't Sunday," Judith said, deadpan.

Richard sighed irritably.

"Oh, come on, Jude. We've nothing to hide."

"OK. Richard and I made arrangements to meet Pete and Deb in the wood on Sunday, for a picnic. We waited, he didn't show. So we ate the food and went home."

Robin's eyebrows rose. A picnic in the wood with Pete and Deb? That sounded a bit cosy for Judith.

"Where were you going to meet?" Robin asked this, thinking hard. She didn't know the time of Pete's death, but she had got to the wood shortly after two o'clock.

"Down by the Farling. Where the pool is. It's lovely there," Richard said, a little dreamily.

"So you never saw him at all?"

Robin thought they must have been in the wood for about an hour.

Judith shook her head.

There was silence for a minute, then Greg asked, "What was his job? Did he tell you in the pub on Friday?"

Judith gave a slight snort through her nose. "If you could call it a job. Mr Tarrant had employed him to guard his herd of prize cows. Some job!"

Silence fell again as they thought about it. Anna's heart squeezed with sympathy for Pete. She guessed he hadn't really reckoned that the job was up to much, but it was something.

Thomas sneered. "Farmer Tarrant would tuck his cows up at night if he could."

He stood up slowly and walked over to where Robin was leaning against a bookcase. He came up close, his height making him loom above her.

Robin didn't move away. She was beginning to learn that with Thomas it was better to look as if one didn't seem to notice how close he came. Anyway, the smell of his leather jacket and the warmth that came from him were not unpleasant.

The time they spent together on Friday night had been revealing. She had found his company challenging, it kept her on her toes. She had to admit that like him or not, she found that being with him was more exciting than anything else she could think of. They had raced through the lanes to Farrow on his bike as if they were the only riders in the world, swift and invincible. He had shared her longing for something beyond the narrow confines of Godmore.

Thomas said softly and with insinuation. "Looks like you were the only person that-a-way, blue brain."

"Sez you," Robin replied. She looked into his eyes as she spoke, and they both grinned.

Anna shifted restlessly. She actively disliked it when Thomas made Robin behave in the same idiotic way he did. She wished she wouldn't. It was as if he was making sure everyone knew she was his territory.

"I don't suppose for a moment," she said, sharply, "that Robin was alone in the wood. Judith and Richard were around about lunch time. We know Deb was there, too, but we just can't ask her right now. Then there's the two in the van. Did the police go to them, I wonder? How do we know that lots of people weren't around? Anyway, the police aren't worried, why should we be?"

"Yeah." Thomas turned back to the others. "Travellers – I hate the lazy sods!"

He spoke with such vehemence that everyone stared at him. His face flushed a dark, unbecoming red and his fists clenched.

"Why don't we all go and have a little talk with them?" he said with menace in his voice.

Robin looked at him curiously. "What's wrong with them?"

Thomas looked as if he was working himself up. "Sponging on us all. Who knows, they may be the cow-cutters; it'd be just the sort of thing they'd do. What good are they? Living in dirty, smelly vans. A health hazard, that's what they are. Let's go and clean them out."

Pete was forgotten as Thomas strode to the door and turned round to see if anyone was with him.

"Well?"

Greg said, without moving from his chair, "Bye Tom, see you around." It was a clear dismissal.

Thomas glowered at them all. If looks could kill there would have been five dead bodies.

"Coming?" This to Robin.

Robin slowly shook her head. She didn't know this Thomas.

Thomas pulled the door open violently, and slammed it behind him. At least, he *would* have slammed it, but it caught in the corner of the rug which rather spoilt his exit. Greg's little dog barked, and the others' relieved laughter followed him down the passage.

The tension they had all felt a moment before lifted.

Except for Robin. Her stomach tightened a little. She had seen menace in Thomas's angry face and in the look he threw her when she didn't side with him. The others were used to him, she supposed, but his blind prejudice against the travellers unnerved her, it was so raw. She guessed it would be a while before he asked her to ride with him again and felt an unwelcome stab of disappointment.

What was it, she wondered rather desperately, that drew her to the man?

5

In the centre of the village stood the church of Saint Dunstan. It was very small, having pews for just ninety people when crammed full. A sturdy stone tower presided over an ancient foundation dating back to Saxon times.

Godmore no longer had its own vicar. It shared one with four other nearby villages. As in many parishes, the old Victorian vicarage had given way to the "new" smaller one. This had been built in the large garden of the old one. Now, that too had been sold.

Some village wits were heard to say the place was now "godless", but the inside of the little church always remained polished and full of flowers.

Robin tended to think of Godmore as "god-forsaken" when frustration with the village gripped her. It was probably the only view she shared with Rob Merton, keeper of the village shop and post office.

This was placed opposite the church, on the other side of the narrow main road through the village. It was tiny, crammed, with a long counter, and behind it, shelves of varying lengths and stability. Tins, packets of all sorts, jars of sweets crowded on to them. A stand of greeting cards nudged up against shelves of stationery, biros and rubber bands. On the remains of the floor space stood sacks of potatoes and attendant scales, along with other boxes of local produce.

At two o'clock, the shop had just opened its doors after lunch. Robin and Anna entered and stood on the square metre of space left to the customers. Anna had come to find out if Mr Merton wanted any more of their fresh lettuces. Robin had come with her for something to do.

"Use your eyes," Mr Merton said curtly to Anna's question. "Does it look as if we want any more?"

He poked a finger towards a box of limp lettuces.

He was a surly man who made everything he did in the shop seem an effort. Which in a way it was, as village life did not agree with him at all.

Not so his wife. Mrs Merton came in from the back room carrying a tray of homemade buns. A little, faded woman, she didn't come into the shop very much as she got easily muddled and her husband snapped at her, but lovely cooking smells would waft through to the customers from her kitchen.

"Hello, girls," she greeted them. Her small eyes, behind her spectacles, were bright with the thought of some small talk.

Robin and Anna were turning to leave, but they stopped to return her greeting. They liked Mrs Merton.

"These are hot from my oven. Take some for your tea, why don't you?" As she placed the tray on the counter she saw them hesitate; they hadn't brought any money.

"I'll put it in the book, your mum pays me later," she added.

Anna asked for six buns, and as Mrs Merton put them in a paper bag, she chattered on. "Your dad'll enjoy these. He's a hard worker, isn't he? Not like some around here."

Robin and Anna exchanged glances. This was standard Merton talk.

"Work isn't easy to find, Mrs Merton," Anna said, gently.

"Maybe not." The buns were handed over the counter and Anna took them from her. They felt warm through the paper, and their sugary smell was delicious.

"But if that poor lad had done something with his life, instead of frittering his time away with that bike of his, well…" she paused meaningfully, "he'd still be with us today."

Anna and Robin felt uncomfortable. It was clear who she meant.

"There's some who say," Mrs Merton went on, "that there were a group of them up there, by the old quarry." She twitched her head in the rough direction of Holly Wood, and added, looking at Robin, "You'd know more about that, I suppose?" The semi-question hung in the air.

"*I* would?" Robin spoke sharply. "Who says?"

"Oh." Mrs Merton looked suddenly vague. "I don't know, but they all say it." She smiled at the girls and bustled out of the shop.

"Come on," said Robin. "Let's go."

Mr Merton had been watching the exchange with his wife, standing with his arms folded against the post office rails.

He snorted contemptuously. "Gossip!" he exploded. His eyes travelled to Robin's hair and stayed there. He snorted again.

Outside the shop Robin aimed a kick at the telephone box that stood beside it.

"That's what I hate about this place!" she exploded.

Anna sighed. "There's bound to be all sorts of talk, you know that," she said. "Some is harmless … some not so harmless…" Her sentence dangled in mid-air.

"Oh? You've heard something, then?" Robin's ears picked up her inflection. "Why haven't you said?"

"Because, Robin, I know you. You always go to extremes."

"It's about me then, is it?" Robin's voice became loud and a bit hectoring. "Out with it, Anna."

Anna walked slowly on away from the shop. "Have you seen Thomas lately?" she asked quietly, trying to sound casual.

"As a matter of fact, no, I haven't." It was a week since Pete's funeral and Robin had grown beside herself with boredom. She would have welcomed even his company, but he had not come near her.

She caught Anna up. "What's he got to do with it?"

"Greg said ... he was talking about you."

"Thomas?"

"Yes."

"And?"

"And," Anna said it with a rush. "And he was saying he saw you in the wood talking to Pete before ... before he..." She didn't finish her sentence but paused, waiting for Robin's explosion.

It didn't come. Robin said nothing. She was battling with her feelings. Anger, certainly, but the one that she was doing her best to cope with was hurt. She knew that it wasn't true, so did Thomas. He was doing this deliberately. Why? Was he just a shallow and malicious person and doing it for fun, or did her refusal to go with him to harass the travellers set him against her implacably?

She felt limp. It was as if her energy had suddenly drained away, leaving her empty. She stopped walking.

Anna, still waiting for her reaction, stopped too. "Robin?"

"You go home, Anna, I'll come on in a bit."

"Are you OK?" Her twin looked at her carefully. This was a strange reaction from her volatile sister.

"I'm OK. I just want to be by myself for a little – you go on."

Reluctantly, Anna did so.

Robin watched her sister's figure turn the bend by the bridge and then she took the lane that led to the westerly opening in Holly Wood. She had not had the heart to go into the wood since Pete's death, but she had missed it. It was her quiet place. It would calm her confused thoughts, and help her to think clearly about what Thomas was up to.

Like the church, the wood was very old. Certainly the holly trees that almost ringed it were overgrown with ivy and very ancient. No one knew if there had always been hollies in the wood. The village historians declared that its true name had been Holy Wood. That had a ring to it, Robin thought. She liked it. Holy Wood; no wonder it always did her restless spirit good.

She hoped it would do so now.

Robin had believed, even though there were things about him that jarred with her, that she had an ally in Thomas. He had loud, hectoring ways when he was with others, she knew, but when they had been alone he had shown her another side. He was someone who seemed to understand, and share, her boredom and frustration... Someone who would give her a bit of lively company and break the everlasting dullness.

Besides, something in his dark, linear looks appealed to her. She had enjoyed holding him round his waist and hurtling through the dusky lanes at speed on his bike. She had begun to think that it wasn't just her blue, shaved head that he liked about her, but that he enjoyed her company as well.

Then she recalled the particular look he had thrown at her the evening they were all at Greg's. She had considered his outburst about the travellers theatrical rather than felt. But that look of his had held such malice and threat. Did her refusal to go with him humiliate him that much? She hadn't wanted to believe he meant that look, but he obviously had. Why else was he spreading ridiculous rumours about her? And why had he avoided her ever since?

The path led into the familiar piece of woodland where she had been painting red circles on the trees. Her eyes ranged around, automatically looking for her work. It wasn't finished, but had, to Robin's mind, already begun to hold excitement. To her, the very hearts of the trees were throbbing with life. She was giving this life to each tree in turn. She could feel its heart jump and beat beneath each completed circle. It had held and absorbed her. She would never forgive the young man who stopped her so abruptly. It was like having a bit of her soul ripped out.

But ... where were the circles? She couldn't see

them, or at least, if they were there at all, they were very faint.

Robin went up to the nearest tree. She traced a pale outline of a circle with her finger. She thought she could detect a faint, familiar smell. What was it?

A movement further into the wood attracted her attention. Someone was there. Robin went on. A girl was concentrating hard on what she was doing. Much as Robin had been. Only this time the red paint circles were being rubbed off, not put on.

"Hey!" Robin said loudly.

The girl turned and looked at her. The other traveller, thought Robin.

"Hey, yourself," she said calmly. In one hand was a bottle of white spirit and in the other a rag. She turned back to the tree and continued her task.

Robin was outraged. Her creative work was being destroyed before her eyes. But there was such an air of righteous determination about the way the girl was going about it that Robin, for the first time, felt herself to be put firmly in the wrong.

She struggled with her feelings, uncertain whether to admit that the paint work was hers, or to creep away.

The girl ignored her. She had her shoulder-length hair divided into many little plaits, some with coloured ribbons hanging off the ends. She wore an old velvet waistcoat sewn with a pattern of sequins and a pair of torn, very dirty jeans. For all her strange assortment of garments and colours, she was at home there, was part of the wood. She made Robin feel, and look, more alien than ever.

Robin's fractured feelings got the upper hand. She burst out, "You don't own this wood, you know!" She knew this was an utterly feeble thing to say, but it was said before she could stop herself.

She was not prepared for the result.

The girl swung round and strode towards her.

"So you must be the *vandal* who did this!" Her face was red with fury. "If I had a pot of paint right now, I'd show you what it feels like – I'd hold it like this." She lifted the open bottle of white spirit above her head. "And I'd…"

To her horror, Robin realized she was about to be deluged with white spirit. She stepped aside swiftly and the stream of liquid spattered by her shoulder and covered her trainers. She grabbed at the girl's wrist.

Before she knew it, they were both on the ground and she was trying to stop her face from being severely scratched.

"Abby!" A man's voice broke across the struggling girls.

"Get off, Abby!" Robin saw a brown hand descend on to the girl's shoulder above her and drag her up. Something warm and hairy put paws on her chest and licked her ear.

"Down, Darwin," said the voice.

Robin pulled herself to her feet. She was hot and out of breath with the suddenness of the girl's attack.

The pungent smell of white spirit caught in her throat. To her alarm, she felt close to tears.

"Let me go, Steff!" This was Abby, turning now on the man. He was trying to get hold of the flailing fists that were pummelling his chest. The dog, Darwin, leaped around them both, barking.

"You pig!" the girl, Abby, was shouting. "Pig! Pig! Pig!" She was beside herself with rage.

Robin left them to it. Furiously, she wiped away the one tear that had been brave enough to tumble down her cheek as she turned.

She had just been confronted with an outburst of uncontrolled passion, very different from Thomas's malicious betrayal, but just as deadly.

That sort will shoot first and ask questions after, Robin thought. Her head was beginning to ache. Ruefully, she mused that she had come to the wood for ease, not confrontation.

Where could she go? The stream and bridleway paths were too close to the previous scene, and she still couldn't bring herself to walk towards the quarry.

Robin sat down where she was, under a sturdy beech tree, and out of sight of the warring travellers whose shouts were now fading away.

Her sombre leather jacket became dappled with the light filtering through the beech leaves, and her cobalt blue head, dappled too, looked like some exotic kingfisher straying from the stream. She had to admit she was shaken, first by Thomas, and now by the physical onslaught of a stranger in a place she loved and went to for a kind of sanctuary.

She felt more alone than ever.

Suddenly the image of Pete's broken body returned to her.

She had been haunted by it for days after she found him in the quarry. Haunted by his white face, with his head at that impossible angle and his open eyes. Surely someone must know how he fell? Deb? Her ashen, grief-stricken face would live in her mind for ever too.

Beaten, Robin gave in and let her tears overflow.

When there were no more left to fall and she had wiped them, and her nose, on an old paint rag in her pocket, she began to feel better. The unbearable tension of the moments before had gone with her tears, and her mind felt washed and clear.

She stood up.

The village was alight with talk and, thanks to Thomas, she was featured in it – OK, that was a fact. There was nothing to say that Pete's death was anything more than an accident – that was true too, but other things were being suggested and, like it or not, she was getting involved. She was driven to the point of madness by boredom – undoubtedly true, so … she'd do something about it. She'd sort it out. She'd make it her business to find out how Pete really came to fall to his death. She'd start right away by tackling Judith and Richard.

Their story was not quite right somehow; Robin

had a gut feeling about it. Deb was still away with her parents, so she couldn't ask her why she didn't go to the suggested picnic. But the others had been with Pete the day before he died, and had planned to meet him, with Deb, in the wood on Sunday.

Brushing away the early beech nuts clinging to her jeans, Robin walked purposefully out of Holly Wood.

6

Anna was troubled. Her sister's strange reaction to her news about Thomas had unsettled her. She felt uneasy. She too had a deeply intuitive nature, but in a different way from Robin. Anna's intuition acted like a large pot of warm stock. Feelings went into her and simmered away for a while. Then, like soup, they emerged as resolutions.

So it was now. She thought about the ruthless way that Judith had taken Pete from under Allison's nose. It was obvious to her that she hadn't really wanted him. She just wanted to prove she could. That had brought all the undercurrents of envy and distrust the group felt about the Londoners into the open. Pete's death, her thoughts continued, was bad enough, heaven knows, but it had made the situation between them all so much worse. Rumours were rife.

Unspoken thoughts were leaving suspicions floating about, waiting to fall on someone.

Anna considered the two Londoners, or what she knew about them. She had seen for herself that Judith was a stirrer. She had watched her seek to dominate the group – and saw how well she'd done it. She couldn't brook competition; that was obvious in her reaction to Robin.

Anna didn't envy Richard, walking, as it seemed, always a step or two behind her. Richard was more difficult to assess. He seemed quiet and pleasant. Greg told her that the boys liked him and she suspected that the girls overlooked him. His build was neat and wiry, and under his red hair his face was pale and powered with freckles. He never seemed to seek their company. In fact, if any activity was suggested, he was inclined to drift away to his computer, or a book. Or so he said, but the truth was that no one really knew what he did, and no one really cared.

Judith liked him around to be her audience, and he liked to be there for her. He let her tell him what to do, and liked to have her make the major decisions for him.

What an odd couple they were, Anna thought. Richard was certainly an enigma, and Judith was anything but!

She passed a group of old stone cottages, the last dwellings in the village. Anna would have to walk another quarter of a mile before she arrived at the line of four Victorian workmen's cottages that included Greensleeves. These stood by themselves, as a sort of village afterthought.

The stone cottages were constructed simply, relying on the width of their stone walls to keep them standing through the centuries. They leant against one another in a companionable way. Two of them were trim and aglow with cottage flowers but the third one had an old rusty bicycle, a bucket with a hole in it, some rough planks of wood and a broken down armchair in the small front garden. Its only flowers were nettles and willow herb.

"Afternoon."

A gruff voice broke into Anna's thoughts. Ted Coombes was sitting in the armchair, with his legs up on the bucket, looking at her.

Anna paused. "Good afternoon," she returned, and went to carry on.

Ted Coombes stopped her by rising to his feet and leaning on the dry stone wall of his front garden. Anna's politeness made her pause again.

He was a man in his early forties. Stocky and strong, he would have been quite good-looking if his face didn't hold a perpetually shifty expression. Ted did work where and when he could get it: ditching, hedging, some gardening and, from time to time, buying local glut apples and making excellent cider. He was well known for this, and was often to be seen the worse for wear from it too. Mrs Ted had left long ago, taking their two children with her.

Anna felt uncomfortable with him. He was a man who insinuated rather than talked. Sometimes his conversation was so oblique that the meaning was quite lost on his listeners.

"Bet your dad could do with some rain," Ted said, nodding knowingly, as if he had inside knowledge of the state of the nursery garden.

Anna smiled and agreed. Again she tried to walk on.

"I like your haircut better than your sister's."

This was too personal and Anna stiffened.

Ted didn't notice. "Someone else likes it, too," he winked. "Someone with expectations…"

At that old-fashioned term, Anna was tempted to smile. What was he on about?

"It's the biggest farm hereabouts, got lots of fat milkers. Better grab him while you can before that piece of skirt from London gets her hooks into him, too. Like that poor blighter in the quarry."

Anna got his meaning and looked him in the eyes. "Goodbye Mr Coombes," she said coldly and walked firmly away.

Ted Coombes grinned and his sly little eyes watched her go, appreciating her slender figure and smiling to himself as if he knew something that very few other people did.

"Lots of milkers," he repeated under his breath. He chuckled quietly.

Anna was relieved when she turned the corner that hid the cottages and Ted Coombes from view.

"Hateful man," she muttered to herself.

A bike came spinning round the corner in the opposite direction.

"Hi, Anna!" It was Allison. She looked far too exotic to be riding a bicycle. Her black hair was bound by a scarlet head scarf and two gold hooped earrings glittered in the sun. Anna felt faintly amused. Allison the gypsy, she thought, remembering how Deb had said she could read palms and see into the future. Well, she certainly looked the part.

"I'm glad to see you." Allison got off her bike and stood beside it; long fringed skirt, strappy sandals, the picture was complete. Anna wondered what she wanted.

"You know," Allison's voice sounded a bit breathless and hurried, "I've always felt that you and I have a lot in common, Anna." She paused.

"Oh?" Anna didn't know what to say; this was news to her.

"Oh, yes, ever since you came to the village." Earrings swinging, Allison took a step closer. "We are twin souls…"

This was going too far. Anna giggled.

"I have a twin already! Don't be daft."

"No, don't laugh, I'm serious. I don't mean like you and Robin – birth twins. I mean, *spirit* twins. I have seen the signs. I know."

"What signs?" Anna spoke a little sharply. She was feeling out of her depth.

"I know the others think I'm touched," Allison

said earnestly. "But I'm not. I have the gift. There is Romany blood in my family – my great-grandmother – and I think you have the gift too, but you don't know it yet."

"Come on, Allison..."

"No, really. Come to my house for dinner, I could tell you such a lot. *Do* come, Anna."

Anna looked at her urgent face and her good nature told her plainly that this, for some reason, was important to Allison. She gave a little shrug.

"OK," she said. "Name the day."

Allison looked as if she was about to hug her, but to Anna's relief she got back on her bike.

"I'll ring you tonight..." and she pedalled furiously away, as if she had to be out of sight before Anna changed her mind.

By the time Anna reached Greensleeves, she was feeling intrigued. She had always nurtured a curiosity about the supernatural. This was one of the few things that she didn't share with Robin. She instinctively knew that Robin would never take anything like that seriously and didn't want her to scoff.

It had never gone beyond reading her horoscope in magazines, and once going to a psychic at a fair. He told her fairly obvious things about herself, and had ended up by saying darkly that she must beware of water. This had not bothered her as much as his prediction that she would marry a rich business man. She couldn't picture herself doing that – unless he owned a chain of market gardens. She smiled at the memory and unconsciously stroked the smooth case of her silver locket hanging in its place around her neck.

Although Anna had never thought about it in so many words, the locket was her talisman. It held tiny pictures of Robin and herself when they were schoolgirls and she never felt at ease if it wasn't round her neck. Just the feel of it there, the silver warmed by her skin, spelt reassurance and somehow gave her confidence.

Still smiling a little, she walked up the path to the back door. She was quite looking forward to hearing what Allison had to say.

7

Richard opened the front door of the Longstaffs' farmhouse to Robin's rather loud knock. True to her decision in Holly Wood, she had walked briskly there before she got cold feet.

The old oak door had an iron knocker in the shape of a hand, fixed firmly to it with ancient studs. It gave a very satisfying knock.

"Oh, hello, Robin!" He sounded startled more than surprised. Robin wondered if she had interrupted something.

"Hi, Richard," she said brightly. "Is Judith in?"

Richard's face, a little flushed, cleared. This was familiar ground.

"She's gone into Farrow for supplies." He hesitated, and as she still stood in front of him expectantly, he asked doubtfully, "Would you like to come in?"

Robin thought quickly. Richard on his own might be a good idea. This might be an excellent chance to get to know him a bit better. Perhaps, without Judith around, he might be persuaded to answer questions more easily.

"Thanks," she said and stepped into the tiny hall. This opened into the shadowed sitting room complete with inglenook fireplace, oak beams and small paned windows. It breathed age and ancient lives and Robin found it claustrophobic.

Richard led the way. He wasn't used to having a visitor to himself. Nearly everyone who called came to see Judith.

They passed into the kitchen. Larger than the sitting room, it smelt of herbs and beeswax and gave an impression of homemade pies and jams. Robin guessed that, in actual fact, any cooking the Longstaffs did was in the discreet, high powered microwave nestling in its wooden surround on the work top.

They looked at one another uncertainly.

"Coffee?" Richard offered at last. He was pleased that he could offer Robin coffee, it made him feel in charge of things for a change.

Having her standing there, on his home ground, made him a little nervous. She looked so unusual, and had such a positive personality. He had admired her nerve when he saw her on the bridge with the others. It took courage to confront the group looking as she did. He liked her style and confidence; it both attracted and frightened him a little.

"Thanks." Robin sat down at the scrubbed refectory table and wondered what was her best approach.

"We make a big pot in the morning," Richard was saying. "Then we pour out what we need and put it in the microwave. It only takes a minute to get really hot."

"Right," said Robin, watching him. They didn't have a microwave at home.

Richard was right. In a minute, two steaming mugs of coffee were ready to drink.

"That way we get real coffee all the time, but we only have to make it once," he said, trying to impress her.

Robin didn't know how to tell him that she only really liked very strong, black instant coffee. She sipped her milky "real" coffee gingerly.

"Great," she said.

Richard laughed breathily. Robin sensed a nervousness about him and put it down to shyness. It was true, he was unused to taking the initiative; he usually let Judith do the talking when they were together. But he was also wondering desperately how he could keep Robin's interest in him, what to say that would make her like him.

They felt silent.

Richard stole a look at Robin over the rim of his mug. He wondered what she really wanted and hoped he had it to give to her.

"Um, Richard," Robin began tentatively. "Have you been aware of any gossip ... well, rumours actually ... about Pete's death?"

Richard started as if he had been bitten and his face became bright scarlet.

Hello, thought Robin, what did I say? She went on carefully. "I'm sorry, I put that clumsily. You see, there are stories going about the village. We, Anna and I, heard some in the shop this morning and if Mrs Merton is passing them on, they have to come from somewhere."

Richard's high colour was fading. "What are they saying? Is it anything about Judith?"

"Judith?" Robin raised her eyebrows. But then, Richard *would* think about her first; he always did.

"No, actually they are about me."

"You!" Richard's surprise was obvious. "But you weren't in the wood, were you?"

Robin thought she had better be wary about how she answered this.

"Certainly, I wasn't anywhere near the quarry, but that is just the point. I can't have people saying untrue things about me, or anyone for that matter, so I have decided to find out the truth."

"What truth?" Richard looked completely foxed.

Robin sighed; this was heavy weather. Couldn't Richard even see the obvious?

She replied rather heavily, "The truth about Pete's death. How he came to fall?"

"It was an accident." Richard's eyes were blank

with confusion.

"Even an accident has a cause, Richard." Robin's laboured patience showed. "How and why did he fall into that pit in the first place, surely you can see that?"

Richard's face grew pink again and he stared down at his hands lying on the table. A wave of misery washed over him. Now he was looking stupid. Now Robin would write him off and he wouldn't blame her.

I've blown it, thought Robin. She had meant to put Richard at his ease, not push him back into his shell as she surely must have done. She had a lot to learn about detective work. How to tackle people for a start. She sighed and prepared herself for a hasty exit.

Richard suddenly looked up. "I found something today," he said. "Want to see?" His voice begged her to say yes.

Robin looked at him curiously. There was excitement in his blue eyes, alongside the urgency. She was intrigued.

"What?"

"It's in the attic. I'll show you if you like."

Robin shrugged. It was off the point of her visit but...

"OK," she grinned at him.

They left the kitchen and Richard led the way up a flight of wooden stairs to the floor above and then to a loft ladder that was standing at the end of the passage. A space opened above it and Robin guessed it was the attic. Richard turned to her.

"I found it just before you arrived and had to hurry to catch you in case you thought no one was home – I nearly fell down the ladder, so watch out."

Robin rather liked attics. She had never been in one as old as this. The roof beams met above her head and then quickly sloped away to rest on the thick stone walls. Robin began to feel excited by the shapes the rough, ancient beams made as they crossed and recrossed the space around her. It was like being inside a living piece of sculpture.

"Mind how you go," Richard warned her. She looked down at her feet and realized that if she stepped in between the beams on the floor she could easily fall through to the room below – or, at least, part of her could. She held on to a roof strut and balanced herself.

The only light in the attic filtered through the spaces left between the tiles of the roof, and the bright sunshine squeezed through them pin-pointing the rafters with tiny shards of brilliance.

It was beautiful.

"Take my hand." Richard was encouraging her to walk across the beams to the far end of the attic.

"I'm fine." Robin was enjoying herself.

She found a spot to stand on the beam next to him and looked to where he was pointing his finger.

Something glimmered.

"What is it?" It was just too dim to see. "Is it a

nest, or what?"

She heard Richard chuckle. "A magpie's nest." He stretched out his hand and picked up a handful of things that clattered faintly.

"Look."

Robin looked. In Richard's open palm lay an assortment of small gleaming objects. There was a tiny key, like the key of a jewel case, a military hat badge, a little shiny mother of pearl pill box, two gold bottle tops, a cracker brooch in the shape of a Scottie dog, and a marquisite earring.

"A magpie, really?" Robin had heard they were birds that collected shiny hordes of things.

Richard glowed inwardly at the thought that he had captured her attention so successfully.

"The hat badge is from my collection," he told her, almost proudly.

"What will you do now, take it back?"

"I don't think so, no. I'll just keep an eye on the pile. It'll be fun to see what comes next, and if it's anything really valuable, I can rescue it."

They navigated the beams once more and clambered down the ladder. Back in the kitchen Robin was about to begin her questions about Pete again when they heard the sound of Judith turning into the short drive outside the house.

Good, Robin thought. Judith too. Now I'll get somewhere.

Richard had a concentrated expression as he listened to the car door slam.

He said suddenly, "Robin, I forgot. Judith and I have to go out now. We have to be somewhere for tea – friends of our parents. I don't mean to rush you, really I don't, but … you see how it it…" he tailed off.

Slightly taken aback by the abruptness of his manner, Robin said, "Oh sure. I'll come another time, and see you both together." She added a little awkwardly, "I'll be off, then."

She headed for the front door just as Judith, carrying two heavy-looking shopping bags, came in. Muttering excuses Robin edged past her and out of the front door. She heard Judith, eyebrows raised, saying loudly,

"What on earth was she doing here, Richard?"

Judith could be so unpleasant, Robin knew she had meant her to hear. Her dislike of the girl went up six notches.

Still, Robin thought, I have to tackle her soon. Not today, though; I'd only be rude and there'd be a row. I'd get nowhere then. Funny pair!

Her thoughts ran on as she crossed their yard. She still didn't know what to make of Richard. There was a vulnerability about him that sometimes made him seem younger than he was. Although, she had to remind herself, he was younger than Judith. Other times he struck her as guarded and watchful. She shrugged. With a sister like Judith, he was bound to be suppressed somehow. Not very interesting, she concluded, and promptly forgot him.

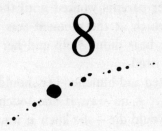

8

The hot summer day had reached its golden afternoon. Robin's watch said half-past four and she felt thirsty. She thought of an ice cream, and then remembered that she didn't have any money. She shrugged; it could always be put in the book and paid for later.

As she headed for the shop, she still couldn't get used to the fact that one could walk all round the village in the middle of the day, or any time, and not see a soul. Was it any wonder, she mused bitterly, that she had been trying to give life and animation to the trees in the wood with her scarlet circles? There was no life to be found anywhere else.

She thought of Anna, happy in the nursery garden, helping her father and blissfully content to watch and tend the plants. Not for the first time she puzzled over the differences between them. So alike in some ways, so close as sisters but, in this fundamental area, miles apart.

A little pang of guilt jabbed at her. Perhaps she should go and help as well. She knew there was lots to do and her parents worked until the light failed every day, which at the moment was around nine o'clock. The heat didn't help and her mother was looking very tired.

Robin sighed and hunched her shoulders. She just couldn't do it – no way. If she touched anything growing, it would die – she knew it would. She'd be a nuisance, a liability. These thoughts took her to the little shop. Even though the door was kept open, it was stifling. Mr Merton didn't want conversation, neither did she. She chose a lemon ice lolly, unwrapped it quickly and sat on a low wall in the shade of an ash tree to eat it.

More like drink it, Robin thought, licking the yellow liquid as it ran down her arm.

Ted Coombes walked slowly past the shop. He paused when he reached Robin and, turning on her suddenly, he said, "People like you shouldn't be allowed in a place like this. You don't fit. All you do is frighten the sheep. Don't do no good to the cows either." He said this with a strange emphasis on the word *cows*.

Then he took a step closer and thrust his chin out at her.

"You'm like some old bird of prey, with your black

,and blue. We was all right before you come. Some of us," he paused and his small eyes glinted. "Some of us," he repeated, "were alive!"

His face creased into mean, vicious lines and Robin smelt the cider on his breath. She thought he was about to spit, but he moved on, seemingly not interested in seeing the effect his words might have.

Robin, staggered by the suddenness of his attack, looked after him. His insinuations were so absurd that she didn't know what to think of them. Certainly, they made her angry, but she didn't feel like having a shouting match with him in the street.

Ted Coombes was right. She didn't fit in. The thought of that made her feel slightly better. As for him, he looked exactly like a piece of the countryside, with his old tweed waistcoat over a rumpled blue shirt and totally shapeless trousers.

But what did he mean by his last remark. He couldn't be saying she had anything to do with Pete's death? He'd been at the cider, she smelt it. Nasty, unpleasant man.

More than ever she must clear up all this destructive talk. It was getting serious.

Come on, Robin, she told herself. Back to basics. Forget the insults, just concentrate on facts.

Right. She had cleared her thoughts. The Longstaffs would have to wait till tomorrow; she'd get to them early.

Rising, Robin threw her lolly stick in the bin outside the shop door and wiped her fingers on the seat of her jeans. She would go back to the quarry. That was the place to start, after all. She hadn't seen it since the day she had discovered Pete's body and she knew that it would take quite a lot of courage to return there. But she would go. If she was to find out what had happened there, she would have to.

With her mind made up, Robin set out purposefully. Feeling a great deal better to have set herself a goal, and pushing her last encounter to the back of her mind, she made for the eastern gate into the wood.

The climb upward didn't seem so long this time. Robin didn't pause to look at the view or the contended cows below; she pressed on. Soon the tree where Deb had sat was in sight. Robin remembered vividly Deb's terrible sobs. She could hear them now, if she thought about it. She dimly wondered if those cries would always be there, echoing in the air around the quarry. For the first time Robin considered the possibility of an unseen world existing within the world she knew.

Suddenly, she was at the pit. As before, it took her by surprise.

The old workings were right at the edge of a sheer drop down to the fields below. She was standing at the highest point of the ridge. The view from it was stunning. She wondered how she could have missed seeing it before.

The flat fields stretched away as far as she could see. Nestling under a range of gentle hills to her left were the roofs and spire of a neighbouring village and its church. The early evening light, now casting long shadows as it bathed the orchard trees and lanes with gold, was breathtaking.

She wrenched her eyes away and turned towards the quarry mouth. Here was where she had knelt and shouted to Pete and received no answer. She knelt there again and the glory of the ridge and its view was snuffed out like a candle.

At the bottom of the pit the earth was dark and a cold, damp smell rose up to engulf her. Small scrapes and loose stones down the sides and at the mouth of the quarry were all that remained of the progress of Pete's body, carried by the ambulance men on its journey up to the light and air that he would never see or feel any more.

Robin wished she hadn't come.

She sat tight and made herself continue to look. Just below the rim of the pit, about a metre down, a small sapling had struggled to grow. Its roots had searched for a foothold in the meagre soil in the stony side of the quarry. Now it was dangling, head down, and all its slender root structure was exposed. Only one fragile root kept it from falling to the bottom. It had hardly disturbed the side of the pit, so tenuous had the little tree's hold been.

Had Pete tried to hold on to the thin trunk as he fell? A dreadful picture rose unbidden to her mind: Pete, struggling to save himself, and the little sapling giving out under his weight.

But he would have been shouting. Why was he

there alone? He must have been alone or else he would have had help. If Deb had been with him, she would have been able to save him from that final drop, surely she would.

Robin shut her eyes to think hard.

Why was Pete there by himself? What had made him come up there?

Why wasn't he going straight to the picnic?

Why didn't anyone hear his shouts?

That made Robin wonder if shouts could be heard as far down the hill as the stream. She remembered she had had to go quite a long way away before the quarrelling travellers' voices had faded.

A thought struck Robin suddenly. Abby and Steff, they were in the wood all the time, they came and went without anyone seeing them. If anyone was shouting that Sunday morning, they might have heard them. Unless, Robin smiled grimly, they were shouting themselves.

She would visit them. She didn't want to, and she didn't think she would be welcome, but it was her only way to go.

Robin opened her eyes again. The wood was so beautiful. Little rustling sounds came and went as she knelt there quietly. A bird perhaps, pecking at an insect under a tangle of brambles, and some small animal scuttling home in the ever-golden sunlight. The thought that it was also the place where a young life had been brutally ended jerked her to her feet.

Travellers, ready or not, here I come!

With her back to the quarry, Robin took her bearings. Her plan was to walk down the hill at an angle. This would make a diagonal line through the wood to the stream and the bridleway where the travellers' van was parked.

Robin prepared to make a route for herself, starting off between two sturdy maple trees. Full of confidence, she began and then stopped abruptly. Her foot had struck something out of place. Whatever it was had given a dull ringing sound as her trainer hit it. She looked down and realized that she had knocked over a large jam jar. It had been full of water and now was lying on its side. The flowers that it had held were lying beside it, scattered by the impact.

Robin bent down and picked them up. Most of the water in the jar had seeped out into the ground but there was still a drop left. She put the flowers back as best she could. They were garden carnations, pink, red and white. Their bright, pretty colours stood out starkly above the greens on the floor of the wood. Someone had put them there for a purpose. Could it have been a tribute for Pete? They were very close to the quarry – if she had been looking that way she would have seen them easily.

Robin put them down gently and turned to go.

As she straightened up, she shivered slightly. She suddenly felt that someone was watching her. Was it the person who had left the flowers? She looked around her. Nothing.

A bird called loudly somewhere to her right, and instinctively she spun round. Nothing disturbed the quiet of the wood as far as she could see. Just a startled bird, she thought. I'm getting jumpy.

Then a twig cracked back in the direction she had come from and her heart began to thump. She began to hurry.

It wasn't easy going. Away from trodden paths, the wood was full of rabbit holes, and the ever-present brambles. She tried to pick her way round the larger tangles of bushes but all the same, her jeans felt as if they were being shredded around her ankles. All the while she strained her ears for the sound of footsteps behind her.

After one particularly difficult encounter with brambles and surrounding nettles, Robin paused to wipe her sweating forehead and get her bearings. She became aware of a low growling noise, in front of her this time, getting louder as it came nearer. She swung round quickly, as a snarling dog burst into sight and flung himself at her.

"Darwin!" Robin shouted, warding off his snapping jaws with her elbows as best she could.

"Down! Stop it!" She seized a loose branch lying beside her and flailed at the dog. He turned, snapping at it viciously for a second, then he was leaping at her again.

Robin began to scream. She heard her jeans rip and felt a sharp fang graze her knee as she beat at him again with the branch. It was rotten and shattered with a shower of useless splinters. Saliva streamed from the dog's mouth as it sprang again. Robin took a step back, tripped over a tree root and fell. The dog was on her in a moment. She twisted on to her stomach to protect her face from the snapping teeth and felt her watch strap catch on a root and break. The dog's teeth scraped against her neck as it took a mouthful of her leather jacket. Robin kicked at it as hard as she could, but from her position she couldn't see to do the dog much harm.

Sobbing with fright and pain, with her right arm bleeding, she had almost given up hope of rescue, when she heard a deafening roar followed by a series of yelps and squeals.

Then silence.

After a moment she realized that the dog wasn't snapping round her any more. She lay still with her head buried in her hands, not daring to look.

"Are you all right?" An urgent voice called her and she felt a hand placed on her shoulder, gently. She twisted her head and saw that it was Steff.

"Are you OK?" he asked her again, looking worried to death.

A spurt of useless anger flooded Robin.

"No thanks to your unspeakable dog! He should be put down and so should you!" To her fury she began to sob again.

Steff watched her helplessly.

He stretched out his hand. "Let me help you up," he said. He was panting hard.

Robin found her paint rag again and blew her nose. She pushed his hand away and, grasping a branch for support, struggled to her feet. She stood there shakily, leaning against the trunk of the tree.

"You're hurt!" Steff looked with horror at her torn jeans and scratched knee. He gasped as he noticed her bleeding arm.

"Look, you need help," he appealed to her. "I'm so terribly sorry – I don't know what to say – what got in to him…"

For the first time Robin noticed the heavy stake Steff was holding. It looked like a fencing post, being slightly pointed at one end. She remembered the tremendous roar and the yelps she heard and turned her head to look for the dog.

"He ran off when I hit him." Steff tried again. "I had to hit him so hard – I thought I would kill him."

Robin sensed the distress running through him.

"It's not like Darwin … he loves people…"

"Could have fooled me." She said this with the shadow of a smile, her anger leaving her as quickly as it had come. Steff, she thought, seemed to make a habit of rescuing her.

"You're right, I need help. Give me your arm for a bit, my legs aren't quite with me yet. My name," she added with a touch of asperity, "is Robin."

"I know. I asked around."

She looked at him and gave a little snort. She wasn't sure if she should be angry or not.

Steff was wearing a much washed Indian cotton

shirt. It was a faded orange colour and as long as a tunic. He took hold of it by the tail and before Robin knew what he was about, he ripped off a long strip from the bottom edge.

"Give me your arm," he said, and came towards her.

Meekly she held it up for him to see. The dog had torn the fleshy part below the elbow and blood was dripping from it. He had also torn her jacket.

Steff rolled back the wrecked sleeve and gently drew the two sides of the cut together with his fingers. Then he wound the shirt tail round Robin's arm.

"Too tight?" he asked.

Robin shook her head. She was surprised and grateful for his care.

Supporting her, Steff beat a path through the brambles with the stake.

"You need to go to Casualty to have that stitched up, and be treated for a dog bite. I'm nearest, but I don't have a phone. You could rest in the van for a bit, though, while I phone from the shop for you."

"I can just see Abby's face if I did that!"

"She's not there, she's gone," Steff said.

"You mean, *gone*?"

"Yeah."

"In that case," Robin said, "I'll take you up on your offer. My legs seem to have gone walkabout on their own."

The old furniture van stood in the bridleway, looking as if it had been left there from some travelling theatre show. Its windowless sides were painted like a pantomime woodland scene. The sky was a clear deep blue and the perfectly shaped trees were covered in flowers and red apples. Rabbits, three feet tall, walked on the emerald grass and a giant robin was holding a singing competition with a thrush. Their orange beaks were painted wide open and musical notes of every type streamed out of them to be lost in the tree tops.

Robin stared at it. She had never been this close to the van before. There was such a feeling of happy innocence about its picture book appearance, so removed from her own darker and more passionate paintings. It moved her.

Steff helped her up the homemade steps on to the floor of the van. To her surprise she found she was a in a comfortable room. A low bed, covered with a richly patterned spread, provided the main seating, but there were two floor cushions and a warm looking rug spread on the floor. Books were stacked neatly on two hanging shelves and a large flat wooden bowl held a mound of oranges.

She sank on the bed gratefully and found it comfortable.

"I won't give you my home number, I don't want them to worry. If you could find Greg Martin's number, Goodland Farm – perhaps the Mertons in the shop have it – he has a car and just might be free to take me."

"Right," Steff waved at her, smiled and was gone.

9

Robin was dozing when Steff returned. It had taken her by surprise, this feeling of drowsiness, and she had given in to it. She'd lain back on the bed and let oblivion take her.

But it had not given her rest. She dreamed vividly. She was down in a dark tunnel which smelled of ancient Brussels sprouts, suffocating her and making her run to find the light. The more she thought she was running, the more she seemed to stay where she was, never being able to escape the dreadful smell. Then a figure, filling the tunnel, appeared, holding out a single pink carnation. Robin, in her dream, knew it was The Magpie.

"Well, you *are* in trouble, aren't you?"

Robin woke with a jump. She couldn't remember where she was, or see whose figure was blocking her light by standing over her. It was as if she was still dreaming.

"Judith?"

As things came back into focus, Robin recognized her. She still couldn't understand why Judith was there, and now she could feel her torn arm throbbing. She felt a little sick.

Then Steff came and stood beside Judith.

"Greg's car was at the garage so he suggested Judith. OK?"

Judith became very practical.

"Come on." She took Robin's good arm and helped her up off the low bed. "We'll go to the cottage hospital in Farrow; they still have an emergency unit there – just."

Robin found, to her relief, that her legs had come back to her again. With Steff's hand to steady her down the steps on the van she walked to Judith's car and was helped in. Steff got in the back. Judith turned round and looked at him.

"You coming too?" she asked, one eyebrow up.

"My dog bit her," Steff said shortly, as if that was explanation enough.

They moved off. The fresh air coming in through the car window was warm, but now the promise of evening coolness was in it too. The clock on the village church said seven. Robin's head began to clear and her stomach calmed down.

"Thanks, Judith," she said.

They said nothing for a while, then Judith said,

"Richard told me you came round to try to grill him about Pete."

Robin dragged her memory back to before her visit to the quarry.

"I didn't intend to grill him," she replied, a bit untruthfully. "But there have been all sorts of rumours going around about who was up there and what was going on. I wanted to see if I could find out exactly what happened at the quarry."

"Richard's a bit wet. You frightened him – not that that's hard to do." Judith's mouth turned up in a little smile. Robin couldn't tell if it was kindly or not. She leaned her head against the headrest and closed her eyes. She hadn't been aware that Richard was frightened by her. Startled, perhaps.

Judith wasn't ready to let it go yet.

"Well then, what did you want to know, Robin?"

Robin concentrated. She supposed this was as good a time as any to hear Judith's story.

"You and Pete were going to have a picnic with Deb and Richard, right? What were you going to eat?"

Judith didn't expect that line of questioning. She paused.

"We were to bring the eats – rolls and that – and Pete was bringing the drinks."

"And Deb?"

"Well, Deb was uncertain, anyway. Pete was going to invite her. We didn't know if she would come, but we catered for her just in case."

"And you were to meet by the pool in the wood. How long did you wait for Pete, and did Deb come?"

"No," Judith replied, "Deb didn't come, and I don't know how long we waited for Pete."

"While you waited, did you see anyone else, or hear any strange noises?"

"Nope to both. I was playing a tape."

"When he didn't come, what did you do, go and look for him?"

"Where would we look? Anyway, I'm not going searching for anyone who stands me up. That was Pete's lookout... We tucked into the food..."

"Without drinks?"

"Without drinks, and then went home."

"Did you notice the time?"

"No, I don't know when it was." Irritability began to show in Judith's voice. Robin thought it must be a bit annoying to be interrogated like that by someone you don't like very much.

They were entering the town and no more was said while Judith manoeuvred the one-way system and drove up the short hospital drive and around to the emergency entrance.

"Look," she said, braking. "I'd give it all a rest, if I were you. You're flogging a dead horse, and I don't mean to be funny. Pete had bad luck. He just fell."

She leaned out of her window as Robin and Steff got out. "I'll be back in an hour to see how you've got on. Good luck," she added, as an afterthought.

Formalities over, Robin and Steff made their way

to the ranks of chairs in the waiting area. It wasn't very crowded. A few people sat around with a variety of minor injuries. A large man, flushed by the sun with hair still damp from swimming, sat with a big toe bound up in a bloody handkerchief. Two children were there, seemingly to have their plaster casts removed from an arm and a leg respectively; one very elderly lady was asleep, a magazine about to fall off her lap, and a mother walked a whimpering baby up and down the room.

Steff and Robin sat down in silence. Blood was oozing through the orange shirt around her arm that was hurting abominably, and she was now aware of a thin trickle of blood that had dried on her knee. She felt it every time she bent it and she longed for a strong cup of tea.

Steff had said nothing since they left Godmore.

"Penny for them," she said, turning to him. Anything to take her mind off her injuries.

"I ... I was thinking about ... Darwin," he answered her, a bit afraid to mention the dog.

"Darwin? You mean the Ravening Mad Dog of Godmore." She saw him flinch and was instantly sorry she'd said that.

"He was fine this morning. I saw him at lunch, gave him a drink and he went off, as he likes to do when it's hot, under the van for a kip. That's the last time I was aware of him, until I heard your rumpus." He was clasping and unclasping his hands as he spoke.

"I had to hit him so hard to make him stop going for you… He just ran off. I've never seen him like that, never. He's such a soft old dog. You saw, you know. You didn't do anything to him, did you?"

Robin prepared to jump down Steff's throat at that idea, but she saw he didn't really believe she had. It was just a question he had to ask. She remembered Darwin's obedience to his master that had made him stop barking the first time she encountered Steff. And the warm, sloppy licks he had watered her face with when Abby had attacked her. Hardly ravening then.

"I didn't even see him coming," was all she said.

"Where is he now?" Steff asked miserably.

The large man with the injured toe was summoned and, limping badly, disappeared behind a curtain. The room was thinning out.

"Roberta Robson," a white coated figure at the door called surprisingly loudly. Robin stood up.

"That you?" Steff asked in surprise. "You don't look like a Roberta to me."

"What sort of a name is Steff, then?" Robin retorted, moving away.

"It's Steffan. I had a Polish mother." Steff's voice rose to catch her before she disappeared. The remaining child, her mother and the mother with the baby stared at him. Embarrassed, he grabbed a magazine and buried his face in it.

The old lady slept on.

*   *   *

It was after ten o'clock when Judith left Robin at her gate and drove away. Her arm was stitched and bandaged and she had instructions to return for a check-up in two days' time. Steff had got out of the car first, refusing Robin's offer of something to eat at Greensleeves. He didn't want to get involved with Robin's family, who were bound to be worried about her and possibly blame him as it was his dog who had done her harm.

Perhaps it was just as well, for Robin was deluged with anxious recriminations from her mother. Where had she been? What had she done to her arm? Why hadn't she told them? Didn't she know they would be worried sick?

Anna looked at Robin's white face that seemed almost yellow against the violent blue of her hair. She looked at her bandaged arm in a sling and the torn jacket she was wearing over her shoulders, and felt giddy.

All evening she had a ringing headache. It had begun after they had stopped work for a cup of tea. She had felt restless and unhappy and knew that Robin was in trouble. She always knew. It was what being a twin was like.

"That dog must be shot," said Mr Robson. He was a man of a few words, liking action better than "hot air" as he called it.

He put down his paper.

"Switch off that thing," he said to his wife, meaning the television, "and give the poor girl something to eat, for goodness' sake." He strode towards the door.

"I'll knock Mr Tarrant up. He's got a gun."

"Now?" his wife protested.

"Before it meets someone else. This Steff," he turned to Robin, "he'll be in his van, I take it?"

"Dad," Robin said, knowing nothing would stop him. "Go easy on Steff. It was a good dog. Something happened to it to turn it like that."

Anna put a bowl of hot vegetable soup with a slice of bread in front of her sister. It smelt good, but after a few mouthfuls Robin pushed it away. It was hard going, eating with her left hand, and suddenly all she wanted was to go to bed. Anna went up with her to help her undress. She turned out Robin's bedroom light and wished her good night.

Robin remembered her watch and its broken strap. It was made of wide metal links and she was fond of it. She would have to return to the wood and look for it in the morning. Then she sank into sleep.

10

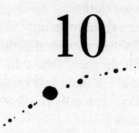

Robin slept late. When she came downstairs the rest of the family were already working in the poly tunnels. They had been pushed into their shelter by the weather. The heat of the day before had gone and the day was bright and squally. Black clouds scudded across the sky at intervals, bringing showers of heavy rain.

Robin found she could use her right hand reasonably well if she was careful. She put the kettle on and took two pieces of sliced bread to the toaster. Her appetite had returned.

The kitchen door hit the wall with a bang as it blew open and Anna came in. Her face was pink, stung by the rain, and her long fair hair escaped its band and waved wildly over her shoulders. These were damp from her sprint to the house in a heavy shower.

"How is it?" she asked Robin, indicating her arm.

Robin shrugged. "OK. Pity about the jacket, though."

"Give it to me, I'll fix it, you'll never know it happened." Anna had a way with a needle and she often made her own clothes.

Robin gave her a thankful grin.

"Saint Anna," she said, with affection.

"No, don't. I'll do that," she told her, as Anna began to get the marmalade and cereal down from the cupboard. "I'm not totally helpless. Did Dad get the dog, d'you know?"

"He came back very late. Said the dog was dead before they got to it, somewhere in the wood. Mr Perry's looking it over; it seemed rather odd."

Mr Perry was a vet who lived and had his surgery in the village.

"Odd?" Robin persisted.

"Well, sinister would be a better word. Dad said the dog looked poisoned."

Robin sighed heavily but said nothing. Poor Steff. Well, at least he would know Darwin didn't just go mad.

Anna said suddenly, "Allison Parker has asked me over for a meal tonight."

"Oh? I didn't know you were friends."

"We're not. But she seemed very eager for me to go. She says we're 'soul mates', or something. She wants to tell me about her 'powers'. Says I have them too, only I don't know it."

Robin crowed with laughter.

"What is she, the wise woman of the village?" She spread a generous portion of marmalade on some warm toast and took a bite.

Anna raised her shoulders and let them drop. "She's very keen. She phoned twice last night."

"Well, mind she doesn't serve you boiled toad and leg of mouse from her cauldron."

"You never know, Robin." Anna's voice was suddenly serious. "There may be something in it. She's been saying she knows how Pete died, or she can find out. She's hinted that she needs me to help her."

Robin stopped chewing and regarded her. If anyone was going to find out about Pete's death it was going to be her. The Witch of Godmore could whistle.

Anna's face was earnest. She wasn't laughing.

"It's all hocus-pocus, Anna. You know that." Robin was emphatic. But she began to feel uneasy: *did* Anna know that?

"Well," her sister returned, a little sharply, "I mean to find out." Suddenly she grinned. "Anyway, it'll be a laugh!"

"That's my girl." Robin sipped hot tea with relief.

Later that day she stood in the village shop. Her experience the day before had underlined her sense of unwanted dependency. She liked going where she wanted when she wanted to go. Something had to be done about it.

Mr Merton glanced up as she entered.

"Mad dogs in the village now! Where will it all end?" He eyed her bandaged arm severely, no hint of sympathy.

Robin ignored this.

"Mr Merton." She addressed him quite formally. "I need wheels. I need money for wheels. Can you use help in the shop? I'll do anything."

Mr Merton made a noise that passed for laughter. It sounded like a plug being pulled out of a bath.

"You'd frighten the customers away, looking like that," he told her. "Trade's bad enough as it is. Come back and ask me when your hair is a sensible length – and colour," he added, as he disappeared behind the post office grille at the end of his counter.

Robin felt the blood rise to her face and knew she was going scarlet. Fuming at his rudeness and sick with herself for feeling so put down, she turned on her heel and left.

"I'll never go there again," she muttered, kicking blindly at the telephone box. "Never!"

"Hold hard. That's me you're kicking!" Steff emerged from the box, rubbing his shin.

"Sorry." Robin was still so angry that she didn't sound it.

Steff, noticing her flushed face, grinned at her. "Temper, temper," he said. "Arm better?"

"A bit." Robin calmed down. After all, Steff wasn't the one she wanted to injure. "I'm sorry about Darwin," she said more gently. "I heard."

Steff's usually calm face clouded over. He scowled.

"If I ever catch the swine who did it to him…"

Thomas swung past them into the shop. Robin looked after him thoughtfully. His anti-traveller outburst came back to her. He may be a shady creep, she thought, but surely not a dog poisoner?

Thomas returned, shoving a piece of chewing gum into his mouth. He paused and narrowed his eyes, staring through his lashes at Steff. Not changing the direction of his look, he spoke to Robin.

"Thought you were particular. Liked nice clean people. I don't know how you can stand the smell, really I don't. Well, one's gone, and one to go. We don't count the dog."

Robin opened her mouth but nothing came out. She was outraged at Thomas's foul behaviour and scandalized at the implication of his words.

He gave her a direct grin, showing a lot of very white teeth. It gave him deep satisfaction to see her so tongue-tied.

"There's a fly in there, my lovely – better not to close it for a while!"

With that last salvo he strode off, chewing.

"Come on, Roberta." Steff nudged her gently, fearing that she would stand frozen to the spot with murder in her heart for hours. "I'll brew some herb tea. Soothing to the ruffled spirit."

"Don't call me Roberta! I can't stand it, *Steffan*."

"OK. OK. We're quits. I won't if you won't," Steff returned.

"How can you just stand and take it? All that …

grief from Thomas?" Robin breathed as they walked down the lane to the van.

"I let it bounce off me," Steff replied calmly. "I think myself into a skin of hard lacquer, shiny and impenetrable, and imagine the words just bouncing off me and hitting the other person."

"Hitting?"

"Yeah, it's quite good fun." Stuff chuckled. "As they are talking, I direct their insults back at them. I visualize them into sharp arrows and send them anywhere I like. Thomas has both his nostrils put out of commission, and next time he sits down..."

Robin had to laugh.

"He said, 'one gone'. That means Abby. Why did she leave you?"

"Well..." Steff spoke slowly, trying to find the right words. "Abby and I, we go back a long way ... five years now. But we only lived in the van for one. Not a good idea. We're like soft and hard, rough and smooth. She's full of fire..."

"Oh, indeed, that I know," Robin agreed.

"Yeah, well... I'm more like water. Moody, quiet and only roused when I think there's really something to be roused about. I was always putting out her flame, if you see what I mean. It was bad for her. She knew it, and I learned it. So, we split. I've just been phoning her, to see if she's OK. She's gone home for a while."

Nothing to do with Thomas, then, thought Robin, thankfully. Maybe he's just all mouth.

Steff had a tiny cooking area behind a curtain at the far end of the van and soon they were sitting on the wooden steps with thick mugs of raspberry and mint tea in their hands. The wind had died away, leaving a day full of sunshine and cloud behind it.

Robin took a sip of the rosy liquid.

"Ugh! How can you drink this stuff? Don't you have any coffee?"

"Caffeine!" Steff sounded as if Robin had asked for arsenic.

Robin sighed. She should have guessed Steff would be a health freak. She thought of the milky coffee Richard had offered her and shuddered. Doesn't anyone drink anything decent around here? she wondered.

Abruptly Steff asked, "What were you doing in the wood yesterday anyway? You go there a lot, and a lot has happened to you there. One, you did those pieces of so-called artwork on the trees. Two, you find Pete's body – that couldn't have been fun. Three, Abby sets on you, and four, Darwin tries to tear you to pieces. That's not bad going."

Robin gently smoothed the bandage on her arm. She looked out over the tree tops and watched the ballooning clouds for a moment. Then she began to tell Steff about her restless longing to be back in the city, her frustration, her feeling of guilt that she couldn't fit in with her family's plans, and how the wood seemed to be the only place that gave her any kind of peace.

Steff didn't speak right away when she had finished. He understood the type of peace that he found in the wood. He suspected that it was not like Robin's peace, but that didn't matter. He had escaped from the city to discover ... to discover... He could not find the words.

Robin's voice broke in on his thoughts.

"Steff," she said, "I'd better come clean. Ever since I heard that Thomas, and others, were saying that I had been with Pete at the quarry, I've been trying to play detective. So far all I have is a tattered sleeve, arm, and ... ego." She laughed, ruefully.

It was a relief to confide in him, and Steff was certainly a wonderful listener. Perhaps, she thought, she could ask him now about the day Pete died without fearing his rebuff. Perhaps, too, he would help her look for her watch.

Absently, she picked up her mug of raspberry and mint tea and took a sip.

11

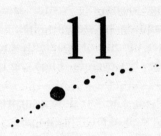

It was seven o'clock that evening when Allison flung open her front door to welcome Anna in effusively. Her long earrings swung more energetically than usual as she ushered her guest into the kitchen. The table was laid for two and a small vase of flowers, stuffed full with pink and white carnations, sat in the middle of the floral cloth.

Anna was impressed, and touched. Allison had obviously made a great effort for her. Her parents, she said, had gone on a week's holiday to France. She had not wanted to go, so was happy enough to stay and keep an eye on her younger brother.

Anna had never seen her brother – she didn't even know Allison had one.

"Oh," Allison told her, as she forked steaming spaghetti on to two plates and poured a savoury sauce over it, "we don't see much of each other. Ian is fifteen. He's into computers and plays games with his friends for days on end. He really isn't a problem." By that she meant that as long as he was fed, Ian took very little notice of his sister.

"We're going to have a visitor later," Allison whispered, sounding mysterious. She shook some cheese on to her mound of spaghetti and looked at Anna from under her eyelids. Then she laid a finger to her lips.

"I won't tell you who – it'll be a surprise."

There was no sign of any "hocus-pocus", as Robin called it, while they ate their meal and chatted together. A fresh fruit salad followed the spaghetti, with dollops of delicious farmhouse cream. After a hard day at the nursery garden, Anna felt comfortably pampered.

"We'll take our coffee upstairs, to my room," Allison declared, as they washed the few dishes and put them away. In all of this Allison was deft and practical and only the flip-flap of her thonged sandals and the gentle clanking of the many beads hanging round her neck marked her out as being different from any other homely, friendly young girl.

Anna wasn't prepared, then, for Allison's room.

As she went through the door, carefully holding her mug of coffee, the scent of incense came at her like a tidal wave. It was in such contrast to the fresh smells of summer and the warm aroma of cooking that she caught her breath.

Allison's room was in darkness. Heavy curtains of a dusky, midnight blue shut out the daylight. They glinted with a scatter of silver sequins that reminded Anna of stars in the night sky.

As Allison began to light slender candles placed here and there, Anna realized that the walls, and ceiling too, were painted deep blue, against which were hanging wall tapestries and posters all full of rich, glowing colour. Above Allison's divan bed, a chart of the Zodiac was pasted and the bed itself was covered with an embroidered Eastern spread.

Perfume from the joss sticks pervaded everything. Anna saw them on the floor, in front of a low rattan table. There were two sticks standing in a painted pottery holder, smoking gently.

She felt she had entered a different world.

Allison went over to her sound system and put in a tape. Low, gentle music insinuated itself into the room. It reminded Anna of water flowing over smooth pebbles in a shallow stream, or of breezes blowing on some faraway shore. It seemed, after a moment, as if it was not in the room at all, but in her head. She rather liked it.

"Take a seat." Allison pointed to a large, soft floor cushion. She reclined on her divan bed.

"This is my room," she declared, rather un-necessarily. "Here is where I really live."

Anna, sitting where she was told, giggled a little nervously. This was totally outside her experience. Her room at Greensleeves was full of light. Her curtains were pale green and her duvet covers patterned with flowers. She had painted her walls with a soft, washed blue and Robin said it was like sleeping in a flower bed.

"You mean," she asked Allison, "when you're outside here, you aren't really alive?" She did not expect to be taken seriously.

"Yes, oh, yes!" Allison leaned forward and looked at Anna intently. Her eyes were large and grey. Under her mop of black hair they seemed to gleam.

"That's exactly what I mean. Here, in my element," she waved her hands at the sequinned patterns that spread, glowing, over nearly every surface, "I can truly be myself. And you can be too, Anna. In this room, with me, you will discover your true self! I know it."

Anna didn't know what to say to this. She didn't understand what Allison meant. Her true self?

Allison was encouraged by her silence.

"You fit in here, you really do." She got up and went to Anna and, taking both her hands, she drew her to her feet. Then to Anna's alarm, Allison, still holding her hands, shut her eyes.

"Oh, Anna," she breathed rather than spoke. "I can see your aura. It is so wide and pure. It matches mine – I knew it would. We will be wonderful together!"

This was going too far for Anna. She took her hands away quietly, and stepped back.

"Allison," she said, as firmly as she could without

being impolite. "What are you talking about?"

Allison opened her eyes and began to realize that she was losing Anna, rather than drawing her in. She sat down on her divan again and spoke in her ordinary voice.

"Anna, I'm sorry. I got swept away by my feelings. Please forgive me. How can I expect you to understand, when I haven't told you, or explained to you, what is happening between us? Now, sit down again, do, and I'll tell you."

Feeling slightly reassured, Anna did so.

"I have researched and studied all this. I know what I am talking about. There is a twin world alongside, or within, our own world. It is invisible to the naked eye, but just as potent, as real as the one we can see. For those of us who have discovered it, can see and experience it, it gives us power beyond all our dreams."

"Power?" Anna's idea of power, outside electricity, was of government, of rich tycoons, of things very much of this world.

"Not the power of this world," Allison went on, as if she could read Anna's thoughts, "but the power of *knowing*. If you have that power, you can see things others can't, understand the future, be in control of so much. But ... only if you are truly gifted, as I certainly am. And so," she added after a pause for effect, "are you."

Anna felt a little thrill of excitement. Her imagination, stimulated by her strange and exotic surroundings, started to race. She felt flattered, too, by Allison's intense attention to her and her assertions about her "true self".

Downstairs, the door bell rang. Both girls started.

"Good!" Allison went quickly to the door. "She's come. Now we can move forward."

Anna, in a state of suspense, waited for her return.

"Come in. We're all ready for you, Deb." Allison held her door open and Deb's small, round figure entered the room.

"Deb!" Anna rose and took her hand impulsively. "We didn't know you were back. How are you?"

"Hello." Deb's limp hand fell out of Anna's grasp to her side. The dim light in the room made her pale face look grey.

"It's dark in here," Deb said. "What's that smell? It's horrible."

Allison ignored both remarks.

"Come and sit beside me," she told Deb. "We have work to do. Anna and I have been seeking the right way to go to discover the truth, haven't we, Anna?"

Anna blinked. Allison went on hurriedly, not waiting for a reply. "Remember what I told you, Deb. You've been away, there have been all sorts of stories going around, and we need, for Pete's sake, to understand exactly what happened to him." She gave one of her dramatic pauses. "And I know Pete wants us to as well."

Tears welled up in Deb's eyes at the mention of her brother. Anna felt an overwhelming gush of pity for her. What Allison had just said sounded crazy, but she spoke with such certainty. Perhaps there was something in it all? The rumours were dreadful, especially the ones about Robin. Could they really find out the truth?

"Yes, well." Deb was having trouble getting her thoughts out. "It was an accident ... wasn't it?"

Allison put a hand gently on Deb's knee.

"If it was an accident Pete will tell us, somehow. I am asking for guidance right now. He won't want people blamed for something they haven't done, will he?"

Deb dumbly shook her head.

"Nor would he like it if there was someone to blame and they went scot-free."

Allison was talking as if Pete was still alive.

"Could I ... could I see Pete?" Deb burst out. Tears were pouring down her face and Anna couldn't stand it any more. She went to her quickly and, kneeling beside her, put her arms round her.

"Deb," she said softly, "there is so much we all don't know. Perhaps Allison does hold the key to a great discovery. Whatever it is, it will be for Pete's sake, and yours." In the goodness of her heart, Anna longed for this to be true.

A small smile lifted the corners of Allison's mouth. Anna was caught, even if she didn't know it yet.

"You don't have to do very much, Deb," she said. "In a day or so, I'll have the answer we need to proceed. You just have to be willing. Are you willing?"

"Well … for Pete…"

Allison took this for the consent she needed.

"Anna and I," she said, "will begin at once. You don't have to stay. You can leave it all in our hands." It was obvious she wanted her to go.

Anna helped Deb to her feet. She could feel her trembling.

"I'm taking Deb home, Allison," she said firmly.

"Come back, won't you?" Allison went with them to the door of her room. She laid a hand on Anna's arm.

"You can see, can't you," she said, in a low voice, "how we complement each other. I am so dark and you so fair. Day and night. Will you come back?"

She raised her hand, palm towards Anna, looking deeply into her eyes.

Anna was transfixed for a moment. She felt her own hand rise up and her palm lie against Allison's; she had no power to stop it.

"I … I don't know. I'll have to … see."

Then she took Deb downstairs and out into the sunlight.

Allison went to her curtained window and drew the thick cloth aside a fraction. She watched the two girls walk down the lane to the village side by side. She smiled triumphantly. She knew she could do it. She would soon show everyone that she was in control.

12

The following day, in the heat of early afternoon, Robin and Steff were standing together at the site of the old quarry workings, gazing out over the impressive view.

Robin said, "Anna saw Deb yesterday at Allison's. I didn't know she was back home."

"Poor kid," Steff replied. "She'll miss him. It's tough for her."

"I keep coming back here," Robin said with a sigh, "but I don't seem to get any further. I'm coming to the conclusion that poor Pete came up here for a walk, or something. Perhaps he'd had a row with Judith and wanted to keep her waiting to teach her a lesson, and forgot that the great hole was here. He tried to grab hold of the little tree and it just gave way."

Steff didn't answer right away. He remained quiet and still. When he had something to think about, that was what he always did. He had suggested they return to the scene of Pete's fall after lunch. He wanted to look at it.

Robin was beginning to think Steff had wiped all she had told him from his mind, he was so quiet. Absently, she studied the fields below them. The same cows were grazing contentedly on the sun-baked grass. Some were sitting down in the shade of a hedge, their jaws moving rhythmically.

She didn't know much about cattle, but these cows were dainty and beautifully marked.

She spoke her thoughts aloud. "Greg's farm is on the west side of the wood, towards Farrow and further. This must be Godmore Farm, Mr Tarrant's herd. Did you hear Judith say Pete's new job was guarding his cattle from the cow-cutter?"

Still deep in thought, Steff grunted. "Um, think so."

"You can get a good view of them from here. D'you think Pete came here especially to keep a look-out for them? It would make sense."

"Instead of going to the picnic, you mean?"

Robin was following her train of thought.

"Suppose there wasn't any picnic. Suppose Judith said all that to save face, or something. Maybe Pete dropped her?"

"More like the other way round." Steff came up for air and turned to look at the herd of cows below.

"That does seem more likely," Robin agreed. "But why should she lie about the picnic? It was such an elaborate lie." Robin ran her hand through her blue spiky hair.

"Maybe," she went on, "Pete and Judith were going to have a cosy picnic up here, on their own, without either Richard or Deb. Then they quarrelled, Judith left in a huff, Pete stayed and fell a little later."

"You mean," Steff picked the story up, "Judith was too frightened to say she had been with Pete, so she made it all up and got Richard to say the same?"

"Not difficult," Robin said. "He'd say black was white for Judith. Anyway, we're bound to find out Deb's side of the story now she's back."

They sat down. Robin sprawled against the warm, prickly grass and Steff leaned his back against a young maple tree. It was hard to think clearly, when all one wanted to do was dream and bask in the sun. Tomorrow was going to be another scorcher, thought Robin.

"Tell me," she said sleepily. "What were you and Abby doing that Sunday lunchtime? Who did you see? Did you hear any sort of odd noise?"

"Abby and I were having one of our moments of peace," Steff replied to her first question. "We had lunch – a wonderful salad of lettuce and boiled eggs and…"

"Spare me." Robin stopped him in mid-sentence.

"Sorry, well, then we put on some music, lay on the bed and spaced out, if you see what I mean."

Robin thought it was a new age way of saying they'd gone to sleep.

"Get on with it!" Robin spoke a little sharply. She wondered why she liked the thought of Steff and Abby fighting better than Steff and Abby "spacing out" together peacefully.

"We watched Allison go into the wood."

"Allison? You didn't say that before?"

"Didn't I? I thought I had. It really didn't seem important at the time."

Robin gave an exasperated snort. "Of course it was important! What was she doing there?"

"She was carrying a basket and looking for things to pick. Wild nettles, elfin berries, shoots of mandrake. She was doing her Gypsy of the Woods act. Abby and I had a laugh.

"It would seem there was quite a crowd in the wood that time – Pete, Judith, Richard, Deb, me and now Allison. Then what?"

"There isn't any more. We saw and heard the ambulance arrive, and then we went to look with the others."

"What others?"

"Allison had come out of the wood and seen the ambulance, and Ted Coombes was there. The Mertons had walked down and so had Thomas. They make a very loud noise, ambulances, and the village likes a good drama."

"No Longstaffs?"

"No."

"Wait a bit." Robin sat up. "Where did you and Abby have your lunch?"

"Outside the van, next to the stream."

"Can you see far? Could you see the other picnickers?"

"We didn't. It is true, you can see as far as the pool, but then again, we weren't looking."

Robin lay back again thoughtfully. It didn't mean Judith and Richard weren't there, but it was odd they weren't noticed.

"If we both gave a loud shout," Robin asked Steff, "do you think we could be heard as far as the stream?"

"We could try, but there may be no one to hear us."

"So true," said Robin and closed her eyes. "Pity we couldn't find my watch."

Heavy black rain clouds gathered once more on that changeable day. The squally wind of the morning roused itself for one more blow. Far below them, the cows began to fidget. Robin felt a large drop of rain fall on to her cheek. She started, realizing she had been nearly asleep.

Steff was already standing up. He was looking down into the meadows. There was something tense about his back view.

"Anything up?" Robin asked, scrambling to her feet.

"I'm not sure. The cows have all just rushed to one end of the field."

107

"Hey, look!" Robin clutched Steff's arm. "There's someone in there with them."

A man's distant shape had come into sight. He was running at the cows, waving his arms about. The startled animals began to scatter. Faint calls of bovine anxiety drifted up to the ridge.

"Who is it?" The man was wearing a straw hat and from the height they were it was difficult to see if he was tall or short. There was a flash of red on his hat.

"It's not Mr Tarrant. He's always dressed in tweeds. We'd better go down. Who knows what damage a lunatic like that might do?"

They turned to make the descent.

"You'd think the cow-cutter would be stealthy and come at night, wouldn't you, Steff?"

Steff only grunted. He was putting on some speed.

They were almost down to the lane, when Steff abruptly stopped. "Can you smell something odd?"

Robin stopped too, and sniffed the air. "Smells like burning," she said slowly. "Not wood, though."

An acrid smell was drifting towards them with every spurt of wind. It was coming from the west.

"Old tyres!"

"It's the van! It has to be!" Steff switched direction and belted off into the wind, with Robin close behind.

The foul smell merged into equally foul smoke, black and thick. It almost totally obscured the van. In the heart of the smoke, Robin could see dull flickers of orange flame.

Steff ran to where he had left the bowl of water he had always put out for Darwin.

"Water!" he shouted, heading for the stream.

Robin didn't think it was big enough to do much good. Pulling her T-shirt over her nose she walked a little closer into the smoke.

"Steff!" she shouted. "The fire's outside the van. Almost underneath. I'll try to grab a rug or something. You keep watering."

With that she moved to the door of the van, leaped the three steps at a stride and stumbled into it. It was very hot inside. Trying not to breathe in the choking smoke, she snatched at the rug lying on the floor and gave it a tremendous jerk that sent everything movable on it flying. Then, clutching it to her, she leaped out again.

The fire was licking at the side of the van away from the stream.

Steff abandoned his bowl and joined her. Together they stamped and beat at it with the rug until the fire was out.

Hot and smutty and out of breath, they stood looking at the remains, relieved the danger was over and very surprised that, after all, the fire had been quite small.

"It was that tyre that made all the smoke," Steff said, finally. "The twigs and pieces of wood and leaves made the flame."

"About a sackful in all," Robin agreed. "Not a lot

to carry, but enough to make a really nasty stink. Thomas?" She looked at Steff and raised her eyebrows.

He shrugged. "Could be any of the lot who don't like us. He's not the only one."

Robin thought of the Mertons and Ted Coombes. She knew Mr Merton wouldn't even serve Steff in the shop.

"People!" She said it with disgust.

Steff was looking at the wall of the van. The heat had peeled off much of the painting on its side. Black smoke had done the rest to ruin it.

"Your lovely painting," Robin mourned, stricken.

"Abby's," Steff said shortly, and went to view the inside.

Robin guessed that Steff's silence was his way of coping with what had happened to him and his home, and felt helpless. She would have liked to say that she would do him a new painting, but was aware that now was not the time, if ever.

From inside the van, Steff said, "God, it stinks!" and he began to pick up the pieces of furniture, the books and the oranges that had tumbled about when Robin seized the rug.

"Come home with me, if only for tonight?" she asked him. "You can sort it out tomorrow." She instinctively knew he would not be going to the police.

But Steff had withdrawn far into himself and she could not reach him.

"Thanks, but no." He sounded remote. "I'm not an animal to be smoked out of my home."

"Well," said Robin, feeling awkward and superfluous, "I need to have a wash after all this." She paused, but got no reply.

"Bye, Steff," she said, and turned away.

13

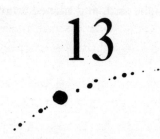

The following day found Robin washing the smoke and smuts of the fire out of her hair in the kitchen sink.

She watched the grey water sink out of sight and hoped that it had not taken too much of the blue with it. What she didn't want was blue-grey spikes. She only had one more packet of the colourant, and it certainly wasn't to be bought in Farrow.

Anna and her mother came back from shopping, then Mrs Robson went out to the ever-demanding lines of plants, leaving Anna to put the groceries away. She went to the fridge and poured herself some lemonade.

"Want some?" she asked Robin, who was vigorously rubbing her head dry.

"Umm, please." Robin emerged from the towel.

"Hey," she said, "you look all dressed up."

Anna had on a clean turquoise T-shirt, and long, dark blue cotton skirt. Her pale hair lay smoothly brushed over her shoulders and slender silver fishes dangled from her ears. Their bright gleam was echoed by her little locket, and Robin noticed a new strand of clear glass beads hanging round her neck. She looked cool and slightly different, though Robin wasn't quite sure how.

"Like them?" Anna fingered the beads. "Allison says earth and fire are her elements, but she says water is mine."

"Oh, does she?" Robin's tone gave away what she felt about that. "Were you there again last night?"

"Yes. She's so interesting, Robin. I've never met anyone like her. Someone who thinks the way she does."

"And how's that?" Robin took the glass of lemonade.

"Well…" Anna's expression was earnest. She badly wanted Robin to understand and be pleased too. She went on eagerly, "She has this amazing gift. She can go into a sort of trance and someone talks through her. It's called channelling."

Robin snorted. "Some people might call it ventriloquism! She should be on the telly."

"You don't understand. *She* doesn't do the talking – a spirit from the spirit world we can't see gives her messages."

"What sort of messages, for goodness' sake?"

Robin assumed a trembly voice. "'Go home, Anna, you've left the gas on…'?"

"Robin!" Anna frowned. "I'm serious. This is important. It's about Pete."

Robin stopped smirking and sat up.

"Allison," Anna went on, "can reach him. Or she can with the help of her spirit contact. She can find out what happened when he died, then everyone would know the truth. He wants to tell us, she says, he's really not far away yet."

"Anna." Robin was serious now. "Don't be such a fool. It's all mumbo-jumbo. Allison is a stupid girl who likes to make a drama out of everything. Stop getting involved in this. It's a dead end."

"No, I *have* to be involved. Allison says I'm vital to the whole thing. She says it will only work if all Pete's friends are involved. *All* of us. You too, Robin."

"You must be joking!" Robin was so appalled she was at a loss for words.

"She's holding a gathering tonight, as a preparation." Anna tried not to hear the scorn in Robin's voice.

"Preparation?" Robin had to ask although she found it all absurd.

"Yes. For the Rite of the Mother on the fifteenth, the day after tomorrow."

"Mother's Day's in March, isn't it?"

"Yes, but this is the Rite of the Celtic Mother Goddess. Allison's channeller is an ancient Celt. He's guiding her through it."

"I can't believe I'm hearing this! Who's foolish enough to go? Will it be fancy dress? Come as the spirit of your choice!" Robin threw back her head and laughed.

"Greg, for one." Anna was beginning to sound defiant. "Deb, Richard, and Judith said she'd get Thomas."

"Judith will get Thomas? Since when did he listen to her?"

"If you must know," Anna knew she was treading on dangerous ground, "Thomas has been making a play for Judith, and she's been stringing him along."

"Well, count me out," said Robin, in disgust. "She's welcome to him!"

Ever since Anna had told her that Thomas was telling lies about her, Robin knew she would never go out with him again. But it was difficult to swallow him going after Judith. Come to think of it, she had noticed Thomas looking at Judith in a funny way sometimes.

Another thought struck her. Perhaps Thomas had been after Judith from the first, but Pete got his bike ride in before Thomas could make his move. Perhaps, after all, his fling with her had only been to make Judith jealous. She didn't believe it had succeeded, but then, Thomas's jealousy might have led him to follow Pete and Judith that Sunday morning. That is, if they had been together all along. But there was no proof of that.

"Allison really cared about Pete." Anna broke into

her chain of thought. "You can imagine how hard it is for her to invite Judith, but she needs everyone who was involved with Pete to be there. She wants him to be at peace. We all want him to be at peace. Do come, Robin."

Irritation rose in Robin. "If you think I'll come and listen to Allison Parker carrying on about spirit worlds in the name of caring, think again! If Pete wants everyone to know what happened to him, let him tell us another way! I've been at the quarry searching for evidence myself, but I haven't found any. I'm sick of all these rumours. Poor Pete died and, if you ask me, the kindest thing we can do is to let it go at that!"

Robin said all this knowing she was not going to do any such thing herself. She was more determined than ever to discover the facts. She would do it her way. She would not tell a soul until she had got it straight.

"Oh, go to your precious gathering, wallow in all that total bilge, if you like! Just leave me out of it!" She threw this at Anna, who looked at her twin's shut face, turned on her heel and left the kitchen.

Robin clutched her damp hair, half in sorrow for their row, but the other half in anger and frustration. Her head was in a spin with it all.

Her father stood in the doorway. "Where's Anna?" he demanded.

Robin jumped; she had been miles away. Her father sounded angry.

"What's got into the girl? The plants weren't watered last night and today, when I really need her, she's gone off without a word. It's not like her, Robin. Do you know where she is?"

Robin couldn't see herself explaining to her father about Celtic Rites and channelling spirits. She shook her head.

"Right. You'll have to do, then. I know I have to take you into the hospital this afternoon to get that arm dressed, but you can be useful now. Water those poor plants and man the nursery in case we get some sales. It's quiet right now, but we live in hope."

Robin's heart sank. She wanted to go and see if Steff was all right. He was so odd last night.

"And," her father's irritated voice went on, "put those groceries away before you come out."

Later, in the quiet of the little office, Robin took a piece of paper and grabbed a biro. She grinned at herself as she did so. This is what all the detectives do in old-fashioned books when they get halfway through an investigation, she thought. Only I'm in a total muddle and it just might help.

She wrote:

FACTS:
1. Pete fell down the old quarry and died. Before he died, he caught at a small tree.
2. Deb found him.
3. I found Deb and Pete.
4. Pete had a job looking after Mr Tarrant's herd. A

very good vantage point for this is by the old quarry.

BACKGROUND:

Pete had been Allison's boyfriend, but now he was seeing Judith who, I suspect, was only playing with him. Judith says they were all to have a picnic down by the stream but Pete didn't come. Deb doesn't know anything about a picnic – or so she told Allison, Anna says. (Those three have been seeing a lot of each other.) Steff says he didn't see Judith and Richard waiting for Pete as they said they did.

Allison was in the wood too, according to Steff. She said she was gathering herbs etc., but could have been keeping tabs on Pete.

Steff and Abby were near the wood. Was anyone else?

QUESTIONS:

1. If Pete was invited to a picnic with his girlfriend and her brother, why did he go to the quarry? Did they have a row?
2. Why did Deb rush up there to look for him unless she knew he was going there? He could have told her he was going to watch after the cattle, and did not mention the picnic or Judith. Perhaps she just went up there, innocently, to keep him company?

SUSPICIONS:

1. Judith is lying about the picnic. She could have been up at the quarry with Pete. Richard is lying

because she wanted him to. She was scared after Pete fell and didn't want people to think she was there.

2. Could Thomas have been jealous of Pete because of Judith? He was the one to say that he thought Pete was pushed. Did he really know anything?

3. If Allison pushed Pete over the edge in a fit of jealousy, she could be doing this mumbo-jumbo to put people off the scent.

Robin threw down her biro. It wasn't any use. She was just as muddled as ever.

I started all this, she mused, because there were silly rumours going round about me and because I was bored witless. I thought it would be a lark to be a detective. I'd give it up tomorrow, only now Anna is involved with this stupid rite of Allison's which is not good for anyone. The fifteenth is the day after tomorrow and I'll never find out the truth by then.

What with Pete's death, Steff's troubles – which may well be Thomas's spite – and the beastly cow-cutter somewhere about, this place is getting close to becoming a nightmare!

14

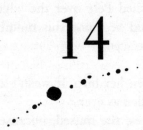

It was eight o'clock when Mr Robson dropped Robin at the mouth of the bridleway after the trip to the hospital. Her arm had been treated with a lighter dressing and the sister told her that it was healing well.

The day had been a scorcher. It was still bright and hot.

She could see Steff sitting on the steps of his van and she waved to him. To her relief, he waved back.

"Sorry," Steff said, as she approached. "I let you go without thanking you for helping me put out the fire yesterday."

Robin grinned at him. "Least I could do, since you sacrificed your best shirt-tail for me!"

Steff said he'd been keeping some bottles of cider cool in the stream and they went to find them.

They were enjoying both the cider and the cool-ness of the wood, sitting with their feet in the stream, when Steff said suddenly, "There's one other thing. I should have said it when we were talking before, but it's not easy to put into words. Abby felt it, too..." He hesitated.

Robin wondered what was coming. She waited.

"Sometimes, when I've been alone in the wood – anywhere – I have had a feeling that I wasn't alone. That someone was watching me." He looked at Robin to see if she was going to laugh.

A sudden stab of memory shot through her.

"You know," she told him, "I'd forgotten, but just before Darwin jumped me, I had a feeling like that, too."

They looked at each other, but before more could be said, they heard people approaching.

Allison and her followers were coming into the wood in a sort of ragged procession. She was lead-ing the line, Anna came next holding Deb's hand, then, to Robin's amazement, Judith was following with Richard close behind her. Thomas and Greg brought up the rear.

Judith, of all people! Robin thought, as she grabbed Steff and pulled him down beside her in a hollow fold by the stream. She certainly didn't want to be seen.

"Hush," she whispered, as Steff tried to protest. "I want to see this. Tell you later. I didn't expect to see Judith with them."

The small group had formed a circle. They were in a clearing a little away from the watchers, but their voices could be heard quite distinctly. Allison was issuing directions. She was dressed in her mourning black and looked, as indeed she was, in her element. Completely in control.

Robin saw her give Anna a bowl and point to the stream.

"We will need water and that will be your task, Anna Waterlight. You will fetch it. Not now," she said quickly, as Anna turned to go. "This is only our preparation for the Sacred Rite. That is tomorrow, on August the fifteenth, the Day of the Mother."

"Anna Waterlight!" Robin hissed in true disgust to see her twin taking all this so seriously.

"What's going on?" Steff tugged at her T-shirt. "I thought Anna was going to come over here and see us just then."

"Just listen," she hissed again.

"When Anna Waterlight pours the sacred libation on to the ground, I, as Earth Fire, will consume the sacrifice. You," Allison's voice rose a little, "Judith of the Flaming Head, will carry the torch." Talking Judith into joining in the Rite of the Mother was Allison's crowning triumph. She suspected it was only to keep a weather eye on her brother, but she was here, and participating.

"What sacrifice?" This was Greg. He was looking out of place in all this. Robin guessed he was only part of it because Anna was there.

"I will bring the sacrifice with me tomorrow," Allison said. "Anna and I will sacrifice in secret, as the Goddess demands, and we will bring the body here for consummation."

"Oh, for heaven's sake, get on with it!" Judith of the Flaming Head looked like thunder, and stamped her foot impatiently. For once she had been persuaded to let her curiosity get the better of her saner judgement and she was regretting it. What on earth had possessed Richard to get in on all this, she fumed to herself. Following Allison – of all people!

"What the devil are you talking about, Allison?" Greg was getting worked up and not to be put off. "Anna's not going to sacrifice anything, are you, Anna?"

Appealed to directly, Anna lost the rather rapt look she was wearing and became her true self again. It was obvious to Robin that this was the first time she had heard sacrifice mentioned. She turned to Allison questioningly.

For a second, Allison looked flustered. Yet again, she had taken Anna's willingness for granted, and now, with Greg's interruption, her precious rite was in danger.

"We aren't going to kill anything, are we?" Anna asked her.

Allison looked as lofty as she could. "The Mother will never accept any offering that does not come to her willingly," she intoned, trying to make it sound official. "My guide, Urs the Celt, will advise us. It may be that Water plays no part in this area of the Rite, and that Earth and Fire are the only elements the Goddess requires. Urs will be my guide."

Steff's shoulders were shaking with silent giggles; he was stuffing the end of Robin's T-shirt into his mouth. She snatched it from him and gave the back of his hand a smack. She didn't think it was funny at all; in fact, she was getting some very nasty vibes.

"Wait till I get Anna alone," she breathed.

"Now we do the preparing of the ground, and when we have done that, I will evoke the spirit Urs to extend his hand to Pete. Deb, as his blood sister, you will stand in the centre of the circle and wait for him."

The group began to circle round together, holding hands and chanting.

Robin took Steff by the arm and pulled at him.

"That's it – I've seen enough. Let's go. If we double up and do it now they won't notice us with all that noise they're making."

Back in the van Steff exploded. He wasn't laughing any more.

"Wicked!" He banged on the floor of the van with his fist. "She's wicked. That little Deb expects to see Pete. What is Allison trying to do?"

"Yes," Robin agreed. "It's very wicked. It's all for her own sense of power. She'll have some reason ready to give, I expect, when Pete doesn't appear on the night. She won't care what she puts Deb through, or my silly sister. I have to stop it."

"Any ideas, apart from breaking it up?"

"That wouldn't stop Allison. She'd only regroup in secret."

"Then what?"

Robin let out a breath. "It's got to be something that would make it all unnecessary, make her redundant. Or even frighten her, though that may be difficult. I'll sleep on it, and I'll try to have one more go at Anna."

"Robin," said Steff seriously, "if you don't manage it and she does go ahead, we will have to break it up. There's no point asking anyone else to stop it; who would take us seriously? Come tomorrow after you've done your best with Anna, and if it's been no good, we'll make a plan, OK?"

"Right. Bye, Steff."

Robin walked slowly home through the now-darkening lanes. If she could get Anna to listen to her, then all could still be well.

The sisters had a blazing row. Robin couldn't remember a worse one. She had to admit to herself that she wasn't exactly tactful. But her abhorrence of the whole rite business and her latent anxiety about Anna's involvement made her go at Anna like a bull in a china shop.

"Anna Waterlight!" She poured all her scorn into that word and watched Anna flinch as if she had been hit.

125

"Spy!" Anna shouted back. "Go on, mock! You couldn't experience anything more spiritual than brandy flaming on a Christmas pudding!"

Normally, Robin would have laughed at Anna's simile, but she was too incensed.

"How could you lead Deb up the garden path like that? You could damage her for ever!"

"It's because I care about Deb and her happiness that I'm involved with this. It'll clear up all the nastiness concerning Pete's death once and for all, don't you see?"

"I only see the damage you are doing to yourself, Anna, being a part of it. You're so wrong."

"No, Robin. You're the one who's wrong. Wrong about everything. You don't fit in anywhere. You never help Dad, you don't like anybody. You look different, you're a misfit. That's what you are – a misfit! I'm going to bed!"

The kitchen door banged shut as Anna left the room, leaving Robin feeling stunned. Anna had never turned on her like that before. She hardly ever lost her temper, but now a wide gulf had suddenly opened between them.

For a long moment she sat in the kitchen, feeling an unfamiliar whisper of self-doubt stealing into her heart.

Everything that Anna had said to her was true: she certainly didn't fit in, she had always known that. But, for the first time, her absolute conviction that she was right and everybody else was out of step was shaken badly. She had always taken Anna's love and good opinion for granted. Her love was not in question now, but her good opinion had taken a knock, that was obvious.

Robin felt very tired. She had come face to face with the reality of death when she had seen Pete at the bottom of the quarry. The form of his broken body would be with her always. Anna and the others had a more ethereal picture of death; to them, it was something they were able to control with incantations and phoney rites. Although Deb had seen Pete, as Robin had, lying dead and still, she passionately longed for their rites to have the power to bring him back. Deep down, Robin knew that nothing anyone did could do that.

She clung on to this conviction as, at last, she followed Anna upstairs and, with her thoughts utterly confused and miserable, got ready for bed.

What made it all the worse was her acute knowledge that Anna was hurting too. Pain of any sort was something they had always shared. Robin ached for her sister.

She got into bed, but sleep was hopeless. The sequence of events that had led them all to this point kept going round and round in her head. Tears were close, when she remembered what her mother used to say to them when they were both little and had had a rare quarrel before bedtime.

"Now, you two, never let the sun set on your anger."

Well, she thought, Mum was right, and we just can't wake up with this on our minds – if we ever manage to get to sleep!

So she got up and, crossing the landing to Anna's door, knocked softly. Not waiting for an answer and in case her own resolve failed her, she opened it.

"Anna," Robin whispered. "Awake?" She padded over to where she could just see Anna's head, half smothered in bedclothes.

"Robin?" There were tears in Anna's voice, and the whole of her head emerged.

"Friends?" Robin gently laid her hand on Anna's shoulder.

"Friends." She heard relief in Anna's answer, and felt her hand come up and cover her own.

Robin let out a long drawn breath, and began to relax.

After a moment, Anna said, "I didn't mean it, Robin. I got so angry suddenly."

"I know. I was getting at you... I didn't mean to hurt you either, Anna."

Robin couldn't say she didn't mean what she said about the rite, but she hadn't meant the scorn and the hurt.

"Night then," Anna said sleepily, stretching out her arm to ruffle Robin's spiky hair. "See you in the morning."

"Night then," replied Robin, softly closing the bedroom door.

Anna Waterlight! she mused as she got into bed.

Not such a bad name for her, after all; it suited her gentle spirit. Then, smiling at her own flight of fancy, she switched off the light.

15

Robin slept heavily. During the night, the temperature had dropped and she woke to find the landscape shrouded in mist. The rest of her family were hard at work already. Anna, contrite about neglecting things, had been first up to make breakfast and first out to start work.

Robin had a cup of black coffee and nothing else. She had something to do and the sooner she got on with it the better. The gathering planned for tonight wouldn't wait for her. She *had* to stop it happening.

Taking her mended jacket from the peg in the back porch, she waved to the distant figures of Anna and her parents and set off towards the village.

She had just about reached the stone cottages when she saw someone coming in the opposite direction. Richard Longstaff seemed pleased to see her.

"Robin!" he said. "I was just coming to your house."

"Hello," Robin replied, not really wanting to be held up.

"I've got something of yours." Richard was reaching into his jacket pocket. "At least, I think I've seen it on your wrist. It's not working, I'm afraid."

He held out his open hand. Robin's watch, complete with broken strap, lay on his palm. She took it from him. "Thanks, Richard. I was missing it badly. Did you find it in the wood? I lost it when the dog went for me."

"Actually," Richard looked a little awkward, "no, I didn't. I found it at home."

"Your home?" Robin was getting lost.

Richard took a step towards her. He looked around almost as if he was afraid of being overheard.

"I've always liked you, Robin," he said, "or I wouldn't be telling you this, and anyway, you've been in our attic and seen it."

Light dawned. "The magpie?" Robin asked.

"Yes, in a way. Only … only the magpie isn't a bird… It's Judith!"

"Judith?" The light went out.

"I feel I can tell you, Robin. You always seem so together and, well, able to cope, if you see what I mean."

"Sorry, Richard. I don't see."

"Judith's a kleptomaniac," Richard blurted out and his face flamed red.

Robin was taken by total surprise. She could only stare at him.

"She's someone with a compulsion to possess things that shine or glitter, even if it means stealing to do so. She's *like* a magpie! I try to keep an eye on her," he added, rather pathetically.

Robin let out a long breath. This painted a completely different picture of the two Longstaffs.

Richard hurried on. "She would never forgive me if she knew I'd told you. But it was your watch so I had to take it, and you've seen the hoard. I just had to tell someone." His words were tumbling over each other.

Robin blinked in an effort to take it all in. Poor old Richard. His beloved Judith was a kleptomaniac. No, she would not be pleased to know Richard had told her, not one bit. This was almost an act of treason!

"Well," she said uncertainly, "thank you for rescuing it. Fancy Judith finding it."

"You won't tell anyone, will you, Robin?" The urgency in Richard's voice was pathetic.

Robin began to feel irritated with him. Really, he was *so* wet, and this was stopping her doing what she really had to do. So she said, a little briskly, "Of course I won't tell anyone. Why should I? It's none of my business." She saw Richard's face fall a little. "Thank you for telling me, anyway. It was very good of you. Now I've really got to go."

"I'll walk with you." Richard's eagerness irritated Robin a bit more.

"I'm going to Allison's…"

"So am I," Richard broke in. "What a coincidence! We can go together."

"Look, Richard." Robin realized she had to be firm. "I need to see Allison on her own, right? I'll only be about an hour, if that. Why don't you come on later?"

Richard was obviously disappointed.

"I was going," he told her, still in his confiding voice, "because I wanted to see if she could 'witch' Judith out of her kleptomania. She might be able to do it. She's very gifted, you know."

Robin rolled her eyes to heaven, but couldn't bring herself to reply to that.

Out of the corner of her eye she noticed that Ted Coombes had left his old straw hat on the battered armchair in his front garden. It sported a red hat-band. She frowned. It reminded her of something, but there was too much going on; she couldn't bring the association to mind.

Richard left her at his gate and she hurried on, eager to make up for lost time.

Robin wasted no time once the front door opened.

"Allison Parker," she put her foot in the door in case of need, "you have to stop all this rite nonsense." She said it clearly and firmly, and with as much authority as she could muster.

To her surprise, Allison opened the door wider and invited her inside. This rather took the wind out of Robin's sails. She stepped over the threshold and stood in Allison's bright, clean kitchen.

"Let's go upstairs and talk about this," Allison said, pleasantly. She led the way to her bedroom, beckoning Robin to follow.

As she entered the shrouded room, Robin took a deep breath. She could imagine what sort of impact it must have had on her dreamy twin and also guessed that Allison would feel more able to resist any pressure if she was in her own sanctum.

"Have a seat." Allison indicated the floor cushion. Robin, refusing to be influenced by the strange beauty of the room, ignored her.

"You are not doing anyone any good by this," she said, firmly. "You are meddling dangerously with people's susceptibilities, Deb's in particular, and Anna's. I want it to stop."

"My dear Robin." Allison was maddeningly calm. "It is not within my power to stop, even if I wanted to do so. Greater powers have taken the rite in hand. The Mother expects her dues tonight and no one, certainly not myself, can disobey her. It would be very dangerous if I did."

Robin began to feel a little helpless in the face of Allison's total possession. She seemed to be sitting in a little bullet-proof capsule.

"Allison," she tried again, "you can't believe in all this; no sane person could. The others don't believe it either, they're just going on with it for a lark. Judith and Thomas are probably killing themselves with laughter. Greg's there because Anna is, and Deb is there because she misses her brother. Anna wants to help Deb and is somehow caught up in all your bogus mysticism."

"Poor Robin." Allison seemed genuinely sorry for her. It infuriated Robin. "So much intelligence and so little insight! You could be as good as Anna, you know, maybe even better. Why won't you try? Do you like my music?"

Robin became aware of the gentle music, flooding the room with soft chords. She began to feel stifled. Allison had to listen to her. This was getting nowhere at all.

"All right," she said, taking a deep breath. "I'll have to tell you. I didn't want to, but I must." Robin had thought this up last night and it was her best shot. She hoped she saw a flicker of interest in Allison's eyes.

"I've been doing some investigating myself into Pete's death. To begin with I thought, like everyone, that Pete's death was an accident. But…"

Here she paused to see what effect her words were having. Allison's eyes were glued to hers; she hoped this was an encouraging sign. Here goes, she thought desperately, as she gathered herself together. Here's where I do some hocus-pocus of my own.

"But," Robin tried to weight the word with portent, "I have discovered the *real* truth and if you do not stop this farce, I will go to the police and tell them all I know. If you stop it, then I will reconsider my actions. It may be I won't have to go through with it. But if I have to, there is not a person, or a friend, who will not suffer, and it will be all *your* fault."

She stopped, hoping she hadn't ladled it on too thickly.

Allison went rigid. Her lips receded from her teeth and her eyes bulged.

For goodness' sake, she's having a fit, thought Robin, alarmed.

Allison's hands moved stiffly out in front of her, palms upwards. She looked like a primitive carving. Her mouth opened and a voice, at least two octaves lower than usual, came out.

"Urs, from the spirit fields of the Middle World, sends greetings. He is the mouth of the Mother Goddess, the Great Earth Spirit which we all serve. It is ordained that today is the Day of Days. The time when the fallen can come to the Mother and be healed. When the fallen can speak again to those they love…"

"Shut up! Shut up! *Shut up!*"

Robin shouted at her, now very unnerved. She knew it was really Allison playacting, but all the same, there was something so weird, so awful about her. The voice seemed to come from her stomach.

Allison didn't stop.

Robin fled. It was all so crazy she had to get out. She flung the door open and ran down the stairs and out into the misty sunshine before she stopped to think. Richard was walking up the path to the front door. She brushed past him without a word, her mind boiling.

Upstairs, Allison relaxed her stiff, rigid posture and picked up her phone. She dialled a number.

"Anna? Good. Listen, I need you urgently…"

Downstairs, Richard watched Robin's figure retreat out of sight. Then he pressed the door bell.

After a moment Allison opened the door to him. "What do you want?" she asked him, brusquely.

Richard looked humble and eager at the same time. "I need your help, Allison. May I come in? You are the only one who can give me what I need. I'm desperate."

Allison's expression changed to one of condescending pleasure. "Come in, do," she said.

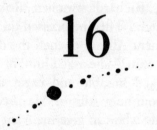

16

"**H**ere's what we'll do."

Steff and Robin were sitting in a field overlooking the village from the south. It was the middle of the afternoon, and they had gone for a walk away from the wood to plan their assault on Allison's rite. Mere threats were obviously not going to have an effect, so now it was up to the two of them to do everything they could to wreck the impending Rite of the Mother.

Steff went on. "We'd better wait until they are well under way – when does it begin?"

"Damn!" Robin said. "I don't know. I never thought to ask Anna. We were keeping off the subject, actually."

"Well, we can keep watch from the van. I expect it won't begin until the light starts to fail. Allison will want maximum drama in the dusk."

"I wish I'd done it a different way. I wish I hadn't told a lie about knowing the truth." Robin pulled up a handful of grass uneasily.

"She obviously didn't take you seriously. Don't fret, Robin; you had to have some ammunition, even if you drew a blank with it," Steff tried to reassure her.

"How about this?" he went on. "We make some torches with rags soaked in meths, and rush into the middle of the group, shouting and wailing. It'll scare the living daylights out of them and they'll run for their lives." He grinned as other ideas crowded in. "We could cover ourselves in sheets and black our faces. They'll think we are some malignant force or something. That would stop it all right!"

Robin didn't smile. Steff wasn't sure she had even heard him.

"Robin?" he poked her gently. "Are you with me?"

"Oh, yeah. Sorry – sounds terrific." She was fighting a wave of anxiety that had come at her out of nowhere.

"Look, Steff," she said, getting to her feet, "your plan's great. I'll meet you back at the van about six, OK?"

"What's up?" It was clear that she was troubled.

"I don't know. I just feel I was wrong to say what I did to Allison. I haven't a clue how Pete died, and saying what I did might have released something bad." Robin shivered. "I feel terrible," she added.

"Now you're talking just like Allison. Are you with me or not?"

"Yeah, sure. It's a great idea and I'll love every minute of it. I'm fine. I've just got to … to be by myself, I think, but I'll be at the van with something for us to eat about six. Don't worry."

"Synchronize our watches then," Steff said, trying to make her smile. "I'll have to do it for both of us – your wrist isn't working!" It was a feeble joke, but Robin managed a grin.

"See you," she said and walked across the field towards the gate. This led into a bridlepath and finally to the lane to the village.

As Robin entered the lane, Greg hurtled round the corner, running like one possessed. He charged straight into her and sent her flying. Gasping to regain her breath, she sat down heavily against the hedge. It was prickly with young brambles which made her wince with pain.

"Robin!" Greg, brought to a sudden halt, looked at her in dismay. "God, I'm sorry. Are you OK?"

Robin, still unable to speak, nodded. Like hell! she thought, feeling the prickles tearing at threads in her jeans as Greg helped her to her feet. Her breath began to come more easily and she prepared to give him a roasting for not looking where he was going. However, she changed her mind when she saw his face. It was sweaty and hot and he was panting fiercely. It was clear that it wasn't just from running hard – he was labouring under some strong emotion.

140

"What's up, Greg?" she asked him. "You look frantic."

"I'll never catch him now – the creep!" he said desperately, casting a glance down the empty lane. "He had a head start anyway. Did you see him?"

"Who? I didn't see anyone. What on earth's the matter?" Greg's nose was running, and his eyes were red. Robin fished in her pocket and produced her paint rag.

"Here." She held it out and he took it, dutifully dabbing at his face. Then he wiped the back of his neck, and doing that seemed to help him feel calmer. He turned towards Robin, his distress only just held in check.

"He'd only just begun his bloody work, the unspeakable bastard!" Greg's anger broke out again. "I disturbed him. If I hadn't stopped to have a good look at her, I'd have caught him at it. Oh, Robin, how could anyone do it? There was blood all over the place... If I ever find him, I'll kill him!"

"Ah!" Robin said, the mist clearing. "You've had a visit from the cow-cutter." For the moment her own acute worry gave way to sympathy, he was so distressed. She knew how much Greg loved his cows.

Then, remembering the red hatband she had seen on Ted Coombes' chair, and the man in Tarrant's field, she asked, "Was he wearing a hat?"

"A hat?" Greg thought hard. "I'm not sure – I didn't actually get a good look at him. He moved off fast in this direction. Why?"

Robin told him about the man in Mr Tarrant's field in the hat with the red band, and also seeing Ted Coombes' hat lying in his front garden.

"Ted Coombes!" Greg started to steam up again. "That dreadful man! Wait till I…"

Robin stopped him. "It may not be him. Don't be hasty, Greg. There are lots of hats with red bands."

"But only one Ted Coombes." His fists were clenched and his heavy breathing had begun again.

"Listen." Robin wanted to deflect him. She could see he was spoiling for a fight. He might get into any sort of trouble. "Listen, Greg, the best thing would be if you went home and made sure the police know all about it, and see if the cow's OK, right? Then, why not slip over to our place, if there's time. Anna would like to know."

Greg turned it over, but Robin could see that the mention of Anna's name had acted like a drop of oil on very troubled waters.

"Right," was all he replied, as he handed her back the rag and straightened his shoulders. "Coming my way?"

Robin shook her head. The old anxiety had crept up on her once more and she needed solitude. She watched him till his tall figure had retreated around the bend in the lane.

I'm beginning to like him, she thought. He cares about what he knows, and is straight and kind. He's obviously devoted to Anna. The thought that Greg would be with her twin at the dreadful rite comforted

Robin.

She gave a little sigh and turned away.

Robin's troubled feet made her take a detour around the village towards the wood once more. She wasn't sure why she felt she wanted one more look at the old quarry, but it drew her. Perhaps, she thought, this time the answer to all her questions would be found staring her full in the face. She laughed inwardly. No chance.

She was right. No answers were waiting for her there. Just the edge of the wood and the fields of contented cattle below. She gazed at the fine view, trying to calm her feelings. But anxiety was hammering away at her peace of mind and she had an overwhelming urge to get back home.

As she turned back into the trees to start her descent, she heard a sharp crack behind her. It was the sound of a twig breaking under a foot. It stopped her momentarily, and her heart gave a startled jump. She peered behind her but, like the last time she had felt like this, there was no sign of anyone or anything anywhere.

Robin, now not only anxious but also a little afraid, went down the path as fast as she could. The safe haven of the wood suddenly became a place of eyes watching her and carried the threat of danger. She scrambled to reach the lower path.

Suddenly, without warning, a tall figure blocked her way, materializing out of nowhere.

It was Thomas. Robin gasped.

"You're in a hurry." Thomas was enjoying catching her unawares. He could see she was unnerved and his mouth curled in a cruel little grin.

Robin had nothing to say to him. She tried to move on but he was right in the way and, as she stepped to one side, so did he.

"Going somewhere?" he taunted her.

"Get out of my way!" Robin fumed at him. "Haven't you anything better to do than to go creeping about in the wood like some kind of pervert?"

Impervious to her scorn, Thomas stood his ground.

"I'm not the one who's creeping about. You've got to look somewhere else to find that one." He spoke with his usual sly insinuation.

"You don't have to creep to be a creep. Move!"

He came a step closer to her.

"I hear tell you know something you have no call to know, blue brain."

His manner had become even more threatening and Robin's heart missed a beat. She realized that he was referring to her boast to Allison. How did Thomas know?

"I don't know what you mean," she blustered, wondering if she should confess that it was all a bluff. This was getting uncomfortable. Thomas would not take kindly to threats about policemen, bogus or not. Policemen were red rags to his bull, of this Robin was well aware, and she was also aware that he was not at all pleasant when crossed. If Thomas knew, Robin wondered, who else did?

"I should be very careful, if I were you. You stick close to that twin of yours. Safer in twos."

Thomas's crooked grin was still in place. He was now so close to her that she could feel his breath on her cheek.

Fear mingled with anger and disgust filled her. She gave him a shove with both hands just about where his oversized buckle met the leather belt that ran round his waist. He was not expecting a frontal assault and staggered back, nearly losing his balance.

Robin didn't wait to see his reaction as she fled from him. She ran, stumbling over snaky roots of trees and branches of bramble overrunning the path. She was out of breath, and panting painfully, but acute terror drove her on. Someone, she could swear, was gaining on her.

The wood became more horrible with every step she took, and still there was a way to go before she would reach the safety of the lane.

17

In the Farling, the young face glimmered through the skin of clear water. This was her world now. It shut her off from the light breeze playing in the air above. Her body rested, barely moving with the eddies, at an angle to the bank. It was hidden from open view by the shadow of a tree that grew above the pool. Only her face lay defenceless in the summer sunshine. It was a perfect oval, pearly and pale, sleeping there like some water sprite.

But she wasn't asleep.

Weeds, counterfeiting hair, swayed to the slow ripples in the shallows round her head. Her own hair was not long enough for that. What she had, about two inches growing between the swathes of shaven scalp, was a startling blue. It could have been some small, drowned kingfisher, except that the blue dye was leaking out, forming a misty halo round her face.

Half an hour earlier the dominant colour in the water had been red. Thick and sluggish, it had oozed from an open wound in the back of her head. But now the water had taken care of that.

She was washed clean.

18

Mr Merton was filling up his shelf with baked beans, inwardly cursing the steady heat outside and the dust that was seeping in through his ever-open door. He didn't like his country business. For him, coming here had been a mistake. If it hadn't been for his wife... Well, it wasn't her fault that he didn't like village life, and longed for the noise and buzz of the city they had lived in before they ventured south.

Someone, making loud panting noises, was rushing up his short shop path and Mr Merton sighed. He didn't like his customers, either. He would turn round and serve when he was good and ready.

There was a crash as someone entered in haste and knocked into the stand of greetings cards near the door.

This made him turn quickly, annoyed, with a word or two ready.

Richard Longstaff was standing there. Sweat poured down his face and he was gulping for breath.

"What the devil's the matter with you – and watch those eggs!" Too late. A carton of eggs fell from Richard's hands as he clutched at the counter, struggling to speak.

Mr Merton saw the shattered yolks and shells spatter his flagstone floor, and opened his mouth again.

"Come quick…" Richard's desperate tone broke in at last. He pointed behind him in the direction of the wood.

"In the stream – Robin – please come!"

"Robin Robson? What's she doing there?"

"Come. Please," Richard begged. "She's – I think she's dead!"

"Bloomin' heck!" Mr Merton pushed up the counter barrier and Richard fled before him to the pool in the stream.

Wordlessly, he pointed.

"Why didn't you pull her out?" The shopkeeper was kicking off his shoes and socks as he spoke. "Help me, lad."

He splashed into the shallow water and, seizing the drifting figure under her arms, he pulled and dragged at her. Richard reached for her feet. Together they lifted the dripping girl on to the bank.

Mr Merton laid her on her stomach with her head

to one side and began to try to push the water from her lungs with strong, rhythmic pressure to her ribcage.

"Don't just stand there gaping! Go to the shop and ring for an ambulance."

Richard went off like a rocket.

Water dribbled from the still girl's nose and trickled from her mouth, but no breath stirred and no answering lift from her lungs met Mr Merton's frantic efforts.

Out of breath himself, with sweat running between his shoulder blades, he stopped and stood up. Fishing a handkerchief from his trouser pocket, he dabbed and rubbed at his forehead and neck.

He shook his head in disbelief at the limp figure on the grass. She was dead, he knew it. He had never liked her, but seeing her like this... He shook his head again.

Mr Merton sat down heavily on the bank and prepared to wait for the police and the ambulance to arrive.

Half an hour before, Robin was standing in the kitchen at Greensleeves. Her head was pounding like a tom-tom and her terror still had not gone away.

She was staring at the draining board. Lying crumpled on it was her last packet of Clear Water Blue hair colourant. Her mouth was dry and fear had made her stupid; she couldn't think. Drops of blue water stained the enamel sink and the kitchen towel was sodden with it, too.

Her dazed eyes wandered to the floor. Long damp streaks of blonde hair littered it.

"Anna?" Robin whispered her twin sister's name aloud slowly and softly. Then her legs gave way under her and she crumpled to the floor, unconscious.

When she came to, her thoughts were clear. She knew she hadn't been unconscious for long or her parents would have come in for their tea and found her.

Everything that she had experienced in the last few hours flooded back. Her terror had gone and her headache also, but in their place had come a huge emptiness. She sat up, strands of blonde hair clinging to her jeans.

"Anna," she whispered again. This time it was not a question.

19

Much later that evening, Robin sat at the kitchen table with her mother and father. They sat in stunned silence together, their hands round mugs of hot, untouched tea.

Did Deb's family sit like this, Robin asked herself, after Pete had been taken away for a postmortem? None of it was real. The only real thing for her was the dull, empty, white hole inside her heart.

"I don't understand," Mrs Robson said for the millionth time, "why she did it, Robin. Do you?"

"She'd been acting strange," Mr Robson said again. "She never used to shoot off without a word. The plants always came first with her. What was she doing, Robin?"

Robin couldn't face her parents' miserable, questioning eyes. She knew, in part, what Anna was going to do, and she had been determined to stop it, so what had happened? Why had Anna tried to look like her? What was that all about?

She just shook her head and opened her hands in a helpless gesture.

Her father stood up with a heavy sigh. Without a word he left the kitchen and walked towards the nursery garden. Her mother watched him go. Anna had been his pride, his right hand; there was nothing she could do or say to comfort him. She turned back to Robin.

"She was wearing all your clothes, Robin."

Robin flinched. It sounded so much like an accusation. Think, she told herself, *think*. Dimly she also felt that this was in some way all her fault, but she didn't know why. She had to think.

She pictured Anna as she had last seen her, in the nursery garden dressed in her working clothes: faded blue jeans and a long green T-shirt. She remembered the way her silver locket had shone in the early sunlight. The new glass beads hanging around her neck above it sparkled also. Was it really only that morning?

"I don't remember seeing her locket, do you?" she asked her mother.

Mrs Robson shook her head. "Or her new beads. Perhaps she wasn't wearing them?" Robin knew Anna always wore the locket, but she was trying to look like her sister, so would she have taken it off? It was such a part of Anna that Robin doubted it.

Grateful for something to do, Robin went upstairs

to look. She saw, with pain, Anna's discarded jeans and morning T-shirt lying in a heap on her bed. Turning to her dressing table she searched among her scattered belongings. There was no sign of either the beads or her locket.

Think, she told herself again. That means she must have been wearing them. They haven't been returned, so someone else has them. Someone who got to Anna before the police did, before Richard did, and before Mr Merton.

Her heart beat furiously. That could only be the one who had killed her. Anna's murderer. Unless the police had got them, her good sense countered. She headed down the stairs again.

"Mum," she said, "the police have set up an interview room in the village hall. I'm going to see if they've found the locket and necklace. They're not in her room. I think it may be important."

Her mother looked at her numbly and placed her head in her hands.

"I'll be as quick as I can," Robin said as she closed the door, trying not to hear her mother begin to sob quietly.

She broke into a run, wishing again that she had a bicycle, and made straight for the stream in the wood. She would look there first.

Long shadows striped the wood. The golden evening light was caught up in the low branches of the trees, making them look as if Holly Wood was lit by glowing lanterns. It was heartachingly beautiful.

Earlier, when the police had summoned Robin and her parents to the village hall and Mr Robson had formally identified Anna's body, they had stood together staring at her still face and the alien haircut above it. Robin felt that from that moment Anna had ceased to belong to them. The real Anna, their Anna, was somewhere else. Perhaps she was back in the nursery garden, or perhaps she was swinging down the lane towards them, but she was not there. Not in that still-damp figure stretched out on a trestle, waiting to be carried away from them for ever.

Sunk in her sadness, Robin slowly became aware that the wood was full of people. She stopped in her tracks and stared. Police... Of course, they would still be at the spot where Anna was found. Why had she imagined that she would have it all to herself?

Robin walked forward slowly. Yellow tape looped in a wide arc around the bank of the Farling. There were, in fact, only three men there. Two figures, one in a tweed jacket, were talking quietly inside the tape boundary, and another stood gazing towards the lane, as if he was waiting for something.

As he saw Robin, he went to head her off. She noticed his momentary start as he approached her. It made her flinch inwardly.

She said, "I'm Robin, Anna Robson's twin. I want to find out if anyone has found her locket ... and some beads..." she tailed off, knowing it must sound a bit odd, worrying about things like that at a time like this.

The policeman obviously thought it did. He spoke to her gently. "Now, miss, don't you bother yourself. If we find anything at all, we'll let you know. Go back home. Your mum and dad must need you."

Robin felt herself being shut out and became desperate. "Please, officer. It's so important... Perhaps they're in the water. I know what they look like. Couldn't I have a quick look? Please!"

The policeman looked at her frantic, strained face, still stained with tears. He knew that twins were supposed to have a special closeness and wondered what this young, strange-looking girl was going through. He turned to his other colleagues within the yellow boundary.

"Come on," he told Robin. "No harm in asking."

He made Robin halt at the boundary tape and stepped under it. She watched as he talked to the others, who turned to stare at her. The man in the jacket came over.

"Detective Chief Inspector Grant, Miss Robson," he said and held out his hand. Robin took it automatically.

There was a great deal of kindness in his eyes as he said, "My officer tells me you are looking for a locket belonging to your sister."

Robin nodded, not noticing that he still held her hand in his warm grasp.

"And her necklace," she replied.

"We found the necklace. It was wedged between some stones." The Detective Chief Inspector released her hand gently. "But we haven't spotted a locket. Silver, was it?"

Robin nodded. "I could look. I know what to look for. May I look?"

It had suddenly become so important to her. Not only to find the locket, but also to stare into the water. To get as close to the spot where Anna had lain as she could.

The big policeman took all this in. Like his colleague, he wondered what harm there could be in letting her. It might help the girl.

"Come on, then, just for a minute." He held the yellow tape up for Robin to walk under it.

She stood on the trampled bank and searched the shallow water for any sign of Anna's locket. There was none. The Farling flowed as it had always done, gently and persistently. The weeds went with it, waving greenly under the water. Big stones, not large enough for boulders, broke the surface here and there and silver ripples circled round them to be carried on and away.

Robin squatted down to get a better view. But still there was no sign of the silver locket.

As she shifted her position, one of her trainers dislodged a loose stone. It revealed a small fragment of something pale. She looked round to see if she was watched, but the men were talking quietly together. Swiftly she picked it up and closed her hand round it, standing up as she did so.

"No sign?" The Detective Chief Inspector came

over to her. Robin raised her shoulders and shook her head.

"Well, if we find anything at all we'll let you know." The well-worn phrase sounded final as he escorted Robin back under the tape again, and bade her a courteous goodbye.

Robin turned away to walk downstream, away from the alien presence of the police. She hadn't really expected to find the locket, not if the police hadn't done so. Nor had she felt any closer to Anna, no matter how hard she had stared at the water. The familiar Farling had no part in her grief. There was no trace of Anna there.

Out of sight and earshot of the activity she stopped and opened her hand.

A piece of shiny paper cut into a tiny oval lay in her palm. As she stared at it she slowly realized she was looking at a minute picture of herself. A younger self, long-haired and smiling. There were two miniature photographs in Anna's locket. One on each side of it, each twin smiling at the other.

The locket had been there. The tiny photograph proved it without doubt. Someone had taken it, probably after Anna was dead. Had they meant to remove her, Robin, from its frame? Or was it pure coincidence that her picture had fallen out?

If the murderer had opened the locket and then thrown her picture away on purpose, he or she must have hated her. First to kill her and then to throw away her image.

Robin shivered. For they had meant to kill *her*, had thought they *had* killed her. Anna had cut and dyed her hair until she was Robin's mirror image. She meant to look like her. Why? What had Anna found out? Did she know what she was doing, or was it just a prank? Suddenly she felt ungovernable anger towards her gentle twin. How could she leave her with this unbearable guilt? It was dreadfully clear to her: Anna was dead because someone had thought she was Robin.

Robin groaned aloud.

She turned to go, when she was stopped by a movement on the opposite bank of the stream. For a moment she hoped it would be Steff.

A girl came through the trees into the open. It was Allison. In her hand was a bunch of pink and red carnations.

Dressed entirely in black, with a black shawl over her hair, the flowers she held against her looked like a bleeding wound in the darkening light.

Robin froze.

"Allison Parker!" she whispered as she recognized the dramatic figure.

Her whisper carried over the water and Allison heard it. In the act of dropping a scarlet carnation into the stream, she looked up and saw Robin on the opposite bank. All the colour drained from her face and the rest of the flowers fell into the water from her suddenly stiff fingers. She looked as if she was turned to stone.

"No!" Her lips formed the word soundlessly, and she raised her hands as if to protect her face. Then she turned to run.

In a flash, Robin realized Allison had thought she had seen a ghost. She thought that it was Robin who had been killed and her spirit was haunting the spot.

"Stop!"

The word was jerked from her as she flung herself across the stream, not caring if her legs got wet up to her knees. The sight of Allison as the mourning priestess coming with funeral flowers enraged her utterly.

She caught the girl by a handful of her full skirt.

"You ghoul!" Robin shouted. "You bogus, unspeakable ghoul!"

Allison turned to struggle free, but Robin, beside herself with fury, kicked her legs from under her and brought her to the ground. Allison gasped and tried to scratch her.

"Robin!" she gasped.

"Yes," Robin panted, finally managing to sit on Allison's chest. "Yes, it's me. How dare you pretend to bring flowers for me when they should be for Anna!"

"Anna!" The fight went out of Allison with shock.

Rage rose like a red tide in Robin's gorge. She grasped Allison around her neck.

"You're going to tell me, now, what Anna was doing when she died. You have to know. It has to be something to do with you and your bogus, bogus rite!" With every word Robin shook Allison's neck till her teeth rattled together.

Terror mingled with confusion in Allison's eyes.

"St ... St ... stop it! I ... can't ... think!" she managed to plead.

Robin relaxed her grip from her throat, but moved her hands to pin Allison's to the ground by her head.

"Think!" she commanded her. "Why was she dressed like me?"

"I ... I don't know..." Allison began to whimper.

Robin's hands returned to her neck. She tightened her grip and felt a dull satisfaction when Allison began to gasp.

"I'll give you to the count of three," she said grimly.

"One. Two..."

"It was your fault, Robin!" Desperately, Allison choked out the words.

Robin loosened her grip once more.

"If you hadn't been so ... if you had joined us and not ... it had to be *everyone* ... and you wouldn't!"

Robin gritted her teeth. She had always known it. The blame was hers. She pushed it away.

"So. What ... did ... you ... do?" A vicious shake on each word.

Allison saw the deadly look in Robin's eyes and began to tremble.

"I phoned her when you left me," she babbled. "I told her that you would not join us now, ever, but she could make it all right by impersonating you at the

Rite. Being your twin she could complete the circle. She could be Water as well as Air – your element, Robin. She only had to look like you…"

Suddenly hot tears blinded Robin. That would have made Anna so happy, the thought of making everything all right, of bringing her, Robin, into the circle for Pete by a simple charade.

Allison saw a chance to get free. She brought her knees up fast, hitting Robin in her back, and twisted herself to throw her off-balance. But Robin was too strong and determined and Allison's sudden movement only served to rekindle her anger. She grabbed Allison by her hair and banged her head on the ground. Allison stopped her struggle and lay limp, watching Robin through half-closed eyes.

"I haven't finished with you," Robin snarled at her. "Who else, other than Richard, knew about my visit to you this morning?" she demanded.

Allison lifted her lip scornfully, but her voice cracked.

"I never took what you said about the police seriously, Robin – none of us did. Richard and I had a good laugh. I expect he told Judith and – well, you know how things get around." She was regaining some of her old confidence.

"You'll never guess why Richard came to see me." She looked up at Robin slyly.

Robin was thinking: she's like a spider in the middle of her web, manipulating everyone like flies tied up in her net. When she couldn't get me there, and I threatened to tear her web apart, she had to reassert her control. She worked on Anna; she knew she was easy. She made Anna prove her leadership by getting her to change into me, like making a dog leap through a hoop.

She didn't answer Allison, who went on, "He wanted a love potion – to give to *you*! Let me up, Robin, and I'll tell you if I gave him one."

Robin heard her, but Allison's words did not sink in. She was thinking of Anna, blithely sure that she was the one chosen to make everything good and whole, walking happily through the wood to go the long way, in the golden afternoon, to Allison's house. Perhaps thinking that she would give her twin such a shock when she saw her. Perhaps smiling at the thought, when someone, any one of them, came up behind her and … the pain of her loss shot through Robin like a sword.

Wordlessly, she tightened her grasp on Allison's neck and began to squeeze. She would squeeze and squeeze until she had wrung every tear from her aching heart. She went on squeezing.

Allison struggled in earnest. Robin's grip on her throat meant business and terror made her fight for her life. Groans and gasps struggled out of her aching throat and her eyes began to bulge. She was powerless.

"Robin!" Steff's voice sliced into Robin.

"Robin. Stop that!"

Robin came to herself. She saw Allison's red neck

163

between her hands with some amazement, and she heard Allison's painful gulps of air.

Steff came over to her and put his hands under her arms that now felt like lead. He pulled her off Allison's inert body. Robin leaned against him, feeling as weak as a moment ago she had felt strong. Allison rolled over on the earth, coughing and beginning to cry.

"She was go... going to kill me!"

"You're lucky she didn't." Steff's voice had an edge of authority to it that Robin had never heard before. "Stop your stupid playacting. It's not only idiotic, it's dangerous. Go home, Allison. Find something useful to do with your time."

Picking up her rumpled shawl and wiping her streaming eyes on it, Allison stumbled to her feet and turned away. She paused once to look back at them. Her face was blotchy, and her neck was scarlet. She looked dreadful.

"I'm ... so sorry ... Robin, sorry about..." She tailed off and her drooping figure turned and left them alone.

Robin sank down where she stood.

"Oh, God, Steff – if you hadn't come then..."

"Robin," he replied, sitting down beside her and pulling her head gently on to his shoulder, "leave it. It's not the right time to be out like this. You should be at home. It's too soon, you're too unhappy."

She let her head rest against him for a moment, then she straightened up.

"I was looking for Anna's locket. Whoever has the locket killed her, I believe."

"Leave it, Robin," Steff said again.

"I have one other lead." Robin spoke as if she hadn't heard him. "I think I know who has the locket. I must go and find Judith." She stood up.

"Judith?"

"Yes, Steff, Judith. She happens to be a klepto-maniac. Richard told me."

She saw his amazement. "It's true. She couldn't leave the locket where it was, don't you see? She couldn't help herself. She had to take it.

"Look," she went on as he continued to stare at her, "Richard would have told her about my stupid threat, right? He tells her everything. She's the best person to know what really happened to Pete up at the quarry, isn't she? Perhaps my threat scared her and she decided to put a stop to me – only..." Robin's last word came from her as a sigh.

"Let me come with you." Robin could hear the reluctance in Steff's voice as he thought about it. This was not his scene, she knew that, but all the same, he was prepared to go.

She shook her head. "If I'm not back by – what's the time now?"

"Eight-thirty."

"Well, nine-thirty, then, bring the posse. Synchronize our watches, deputy!"

Steff tried to grin weakly. Then he said, "Wait. I remember I saw Judith walking up the bridleway about half an hour ago. Thomas was with her. She may not be at home."

"If she isn't, I'll get it out of Richard if he's around. He won't be difficult. I think he's got a thing about me."

Steff was looking worried, so Robin forced a smile. "Wish me luck. I'll tread carefully, never fear!" She waved what she hoped was a cheery hand at him. He stood still, anxiously watching her go.

20

The attic of the old farmhouse was almost completely dark. Although dusk was settling on Godmore, making the summer trees look black against a washed turquoise sky, there was still a lot of light outside. Not much of it, however, penetrated the tiled roof space, and what did was squeezed into tiny patches of blue haze.

Robin, perched on two crossbeams, peered into the corner where she had seen the "magpie's hoard" with Richard.

The house was deserted when she arrived at the front door. No lights were on, although Judith's car was standing in the yard. There was no sign of Richard, either.

Robin hesitated for a moment, then, going round to the back of the house, she tried the handle of the back door. It wasn't locked. She slipped inside, seeing the shapes of coats on pegs and avoiding a line of gumboots on the flagged floor.

In the kitchen she stood still and listened. She heard only the ticking of the clock on the wall, and the far-off creak of wooden joints in the ancient beams. She smoothed her bandaged arm gently. All the activity with Allison had left it throbbing.

She would look in the attic. If the locket wasn't there, well, no harm had been done and it was better that she hadn't accused Judith of taking it.

Precariously balanced, she knelt so that she could reach down to where the small pile of objects lay, glimmering faintly. Gingerly she put out a feeling hand. Her fingers touched something round and smooth; groping further they entwined themselves in a slender chain. Anna's locket was there. Her heart gave a sudden leap and her head swam as she picked it up. If she left it where it was, it could easily be gone by the time she could get the police there. It was her only evidence; she had to take it with her.

As she rose, her foot slipped off the beam. It landed on the thin skin of paper and plaster that was the ceiling of the room below. There was an ominous cracking sound as pieces of loosened plaster fell on to the furniture beneath. Mercifully, her foot did not go through.

Robin froze and listened hard. Far away in the house a door opened and shut. Footsteps came hurrying up the stairs. Someone was back and had heard the noise. Robin prayed it was Richard.

She was trapped. There was only one opening to the attic floor and the footsteps were arriving at the bottom of the loft ladder. Whoever it was had stopped there to listen.

Then they began to climb.

Robin decided on action. If she allowed herself to be discovered in the attic there was no room for manoeuvre. If she surprised whoever it was while they were also in a vulnerable position, like halfway up a ladder, there was a chance that she could knock them over and make a run for it.

She took a deep breath and warily made for the opening. In a flash she had flung her legs over the side and began to get the rest of her body after them. She was not prepared for the terrified scream that met her as she stood revealed on the ladder.

Judith, her mouth wide open and face as white as a sheet, loosened her grip on the ladder and fell backwards.

"You!" she gasped at Robin.

Registering that Judith had more reason than Allison to think that she was dead, Robin clambered down the rest of the ladder and gave her a hard shove. She intended to use shock tactics to escape down the stairs and out to the police.

Judith saw Anna's locket dangling from Robin's fist. The sight of it and its implications made her act fast. Swiftly, she recovered herself and seized Robin by the arm. It was Robin's wounded arm and she cried out.

Seeing her advantage, Judith tightened her grip. Robin's instinct was to relax to try to lessen the searing pain. With her other hand she caught at Judith's long, flaming red plait, pulling it hard.

Judith yelled, and her eyes watered, but she would not let Robin go. She tried to twist the locket out of Robin's grasp. It was dangling from her right hand, her injured arm.

"Let … it … go!" Judith hissed in her ear. "You are not going to tell anyone … ever!" The locket wrenched free.

Robin believed her. If Judith had her way she would not be telling anyone anything. Judith looked and sounded crazy. Pain from her arm was all that she could feel, but the loss of Anna's locket was like a part of her self being cut away. Robin made a final effort.

Trying hard to blot out the agony, she managed to twist her arm free from Judith's grasp. She swung round, twined her legs behind Judith's knees and took her off her balance. There was not enough room in the narrow corridor for Judith to fall, so Robin pinned her head against the wall with her good elbow across her neck. She kneed her in the stomach hard and Judith doubled over, winded.

Gasping and helpless, Robin dragged her into the nearest bedroom. It was unoccupied. Seeing a large wardrobe, she jerked it open and bundled the still-retching Judith inside. It was a tight fit, but Robin got the door closed and turned the slender key. She rushed to the corridor, pulled a small oak chest against the door and made for the stairs.

Richard was standing at the bottom.

The pain in Robin's arm threatened to engulf her and her vision clouded. Richard, she thought. Thank God!

Richard saw her sway and came up towards her. He moved slowly, his face against his red hair very white. Dimly Robin knew he too was suffering the shock of seeing her. He had found her dead body, after all. She strove to remain on her feet to reassure him, leaning against the wall for support.

"It's me all right, Richard – Robin," Robin began. "It was Anna you found in the stream, dressed like me. I'm really Robin. I'm alive..." Only just, her mind said.

"Anna?" Richard was struggling to adjust.

Banging came from the spare room. Judith had recovered her breath.

Robin said hurriedly, "Tell you later. Got to get to the police, Richard... That's Judith – I've shut her in a cupboard..." She suddenly realized the effect this might have on a devoted Richard and hesitated, but then went on doggedly.

"She's a killer, Richard. I had to shut her in. She must have murdered Pete, and now she's killed Anna. She thought it was me, but it was Anna. We must go... *Now!*" She shouted suddenly as Richard seemed dazed and the banging was getting frantic. The cupboard would not hold Judith for long.

"Judith." Richard didn't sound surprised. He sounded calm and in control. "I know. I saw her push Pete. She didn't know I was there – but she is my sister. You wouldn't tell on your sister, would you, Robin?"

Robin couldn't think. Everything was going too quickly for her. So Richard had known about Judith all along?

Richard was still talking as if he'd never stop.

"I guessed about … the other one, when I saw the locket in her hoard. Anna wasn't wearing it when I found her in the stream, but then I didn't know she wasn't you. I didn't know she might have worn it … earlier… I didn't know what to do when I found it, Robin…" Suddenly his face crumpled into a small child's lost one.

Robin tried to rally him.

"I know it's terrible for you, Richard – but we must go to the police in the village hall. Or we must phone them. Just listen to her – she'll be out in a second. Come *on*!"

Richard was blocking her way. He looked into her face now and his hand came up to touch her hair.

"I'm glad it wasn't you I found, Robin," he said, still like a child who had been let off a punishment. "I really like being with you. You're strong, like Judith, but so much nicer…" His hand began to stroke her face.

"For God's sake, Richard!" He must be suffering

from combined shock, she thought, but her instinctive reaction was to push him away. Horrified, she watched him slip and tumble down the short flight of stairs to the floor. She went quickly down to try and help him up.

"Are you OK?" she asked him anxiously, with her good arm about to take his hand. "I didn't mean…" but her voice tailed off as Richard lifted his head and his pale eyes looked at her.

They were blazing. He rose up to a crouching position, and Robin saw, with disbelief, that he had a flick knife in his hand. The blade was out, pointing at her.

Robin went icy cold. Richard, not Judith! She had shut the wrong person in the cupboard! She saw him grin. There was a crazy kind of triumph in it.

"No one pushes me away," he said softly. The pure hatred in his eyes drenched her.

"That was the trouble with Pete, you see." Richard's voice was deadly quiet. "He always tried to push me away, to have Judith to himself."

The grin remained but the eyes spoke their hatred.

"That's what he did that Sunday. They didn't ask me along to their picnic, so I followed them up to the quarry. His precious cattle-watching job!" Richard's voice was full of contempt. "Judith made me say I was with her all the time afterwards. She was scared." He almost gloated.

Robin's frozen mind refused to work.

"*You* pushed Pete?" she asked stupidly.

, Richard's mouth turned up at the edges, making his ugly grin even uglier. Robin shuddered.

"They laid it on for me," he said. "They had a row and Judith shoved him. He slipped over the edge. She was furious, so she just turned her back and left him there. He was hanging on to something, half in, half scrambling out. He was so cross and he looked so silly."

"You mean he wasn't in danger then? He could get out?" The little sapling, thought Robin. He was safe hanging on to that.

"Oh, he was very pleased to see me," she heard Richard chuckle. "'Give us a hand up, Richard,' and all that. All I had to do was give a good hard push. It was so easy. He didn't even have time to shout."

"Poor Pete," Robin's stiff lips could only just form the words. The world around her was threatening to recede again. She held her wounded arm close to her chest and realized that it was bleeding through the bandage.

Richard recognized her weakness and moved closer. His knife point was about a foot away from her stomach.

"But I thought you knew all that, Robin. Isn't that what you were going to tell the police if Allison went ahead with her plan?"

"I didn't know anything," Robin managed to gasp. "I was bluffing." She remembered something and grasped at it. "You went to Allison for a love potion, didn't you? A love potion for me, Richard. You wouldn't hurt me, you like me, and I … like you. I won't tell anyone."

"Too late, Robin." Richard shook his head at her. "A moment ago perhaps … but I had to stop you then, and I did, didn't I? I hit you on the head and put you in the stream – that stopped you … dead!" Through the gathering mist around her, Robin heard him giggle.

"I'm going to have to stop you again."

The knocker on the farmhouse door burst into life.

Richard grabbed her round the neck and brought the knife close up under her chin.

"Don't even breathe!" he hissed in her ear.

Upstairs, the frantic bangings had dropped to a steady thump.

Another burst of knocking on the front door filled the house. Richard dragged the helpless Robin into the kitchen and made her crouch with him beside the table. The light had all gone now and the room was very dark. Robin remembered the unlocked back door and prayed silently that whoever was knocking so hard would go round that way and find it.

They did not have long to wait. The back door flew open and, with a crash, Steff burst into the kitchen.

Richard tightened his hold on Robin and the knife point pricked her throat.

Light flooded the room as Steff flicked the switch.

Overcome with fear and pain, Robin fainted.

When she opened her eyes again, she was lying on the matting that covered the flagstones of the kitchen floor. Steff was sitting astride Richard's back and he was tying Richard's hands behind him with strips from a linen tea towel. The flick knife was nowhere to be seen.

As if in a dream, she watched Steff expertly finish with Richard's hands and then get off him. He looped another length of towel around the bonds and then round a leg of the heavy refectory table. Richard was secure. His pale face under his dishevelled red hair looked young and somehow blank. He seemed stunned, as if he had lost his powers of speech.

Then Steff turned to look at her. When he saw that she was conscious again, he lifted her gently into a sitting position.

"Do you realize," Robin asked him weakly, "that you have rescued me again?"

"Habit," said Steff.

Judith came in from the hall. The latch on the cupboard door had finally given under her blows, and let her out. Robin and Steff stared at her as if she was a stranger. They had forgotten she was up there. How long had she been free? What had she heard?

Deathly white, she sat down heavily at the kitchen table.

"I've phoned the police," she said, without emotion. "They're coming."

"Hot, sweet tea," said Steff.

Judith rose obediently. As she filled the kettle and

went about the simple everyday tasks, getting mugs and the teapot from a cupboard, she said, again without any feeling, "I knew about Richard, you know. Or rather, I guessed about Pete, but I was too frightened for myself to say anything. And, after all … he's…" She stopped.

"Your brother," Robin finished it for her. Judith turned and looked directly at her.

"About the locket, Robin." She wet her lips and cleared a throat that threatened to dry up. It was obvious to the other two that this was not going to be easy for her.

"I had sent Richard for some eggs from Mrs Grieves, and he was a long time away, so I went out to find him. He takes to wandering, you know, and can be gone for hours." She spooned some tea into the pot.

Robin could see she was playing for time. Her hand holding the tea caddy was shaking badly.

"I saw Anna in the stream." Judith's voice was still calm, but she put the tea caddy down and grasped both her hands together to try to stop them trembling. "She was dead, so I couldn't help her." She looked away and went on almost under her breath.

"Richard must have gone for the eggs after he had killed her."

Robin sucked in her breath at the cold-blooded act. He had killed, and gone on to buy eggs. Then he returned to "find" her body so no one would connect him with the murder. She shivered.

Judith was still speaking. "I felt so sick. Sick because I found her and sick because, at the time, I didn't dare think who had killed her. I thought she was you, Robin. And sick ... sick ... because I wanted the locket more than all that put together. I never wondered why you were wearing it, not Anna – I just had to have it." The whole of her body was shaking. Judith sank on to the nearest chair and wept openly.

"Now everybody will know about me," she sobbed desperately, tears streaming down her face, "and I can't help it. I can't..." Like a little girl, she buried her wet face in her hands and howled.

Headlights from the police car flickered on the window glass as it drove into the drive with a spurt of gravel.

Steff, hearing the car doors slam, rose and went to open the front door with a heavy sigh.

21

Robin sat silently with Steff on the steps of his van. It was their first proper meeting since Anna's funeral. A sense of sadness hung over them like a cloud.

"Longstaffs' house is up for sale." Steff spoke quietly.

"Hmm, I know." Robin sighed. "Poor Judith."

"Poor Judith?" Steff questioned her.

"You know what the tabloid papers did. They crucified her parents, and you know what they said about her. I can't imagine what it's like to be in her shoes now."

Silence fell between them again.

"I never asked you," Robin said at last, "why you came to find me. I hadn't been gone over an hour, had I?"

"Ah, well," Steff seemed reluctant to tell her. "I found Thomas spraying the side of my van. I think he was spraying the word VERMIN, but he'd only got as far as the letter R."

"What on earth has Thomas got to do with anything, Steff?"

"Well, when I saw him at it, I sort of lost my cool. It was the last straw. After poor old Darwin and the fire and everything." Steff didn't really didn't want to say any more.

Robin was ruthless.

"So?" She prodded him gently, admitting to herself that she would have given anything to see Steff lose his cool at last.

Steff sighed. There was no way out.

"I'm ... a karate black belt," he said sheepishly.

"You!"

Steff was blushing and Robin tried not to grin at his obvious discomfort.

"So?" she prompted him.

"So, when I was sitting on Thomas's head, and I was accusing him of killing my dog and setting my home on fire and creeping about spying on people and probably knowing all along what exactly happened to Pete, I got it out of him."

"OK. What?" Robin was enjoying the picture that Steff's story presented, of a helpless, supine Thomas getting exactly what he deserved.

"The only thing he could deny was being the creeper. When you and I felt we were being watched in the wood, it was because we were. Richard was stalking us. Thomas said he had seen him at it often. Well, Thomas is a boaster, but that was probably true. Knowing Richard as we do now, we know he would relish the thought that he could see, but not be seen himself. We know he needed to get power over people somehow. Learning their secrets by spying on them was one way of getting it." Steff stopped again, as if he had made it all plain.

"But what made you come to look for me?" Robin insisted.

"Because, between a stalker and a kleptomaniac, with two weird deaths in the village, it seemed to me you might need help."

Robin looked into his earnest brown eyes and put two and two together.

"Poor old Richard," she said quietly. "He didn't have a chance against a karate black belt – thank goodness!"

For a while longer they sat quietly with their arms around each other's shoulders. Robin knew there was no need to embarrass Steff more by thanking him, but gratitude swelled in her.

Out of the blue, Steff said, "You know Greg caught the cow-cutter?"

"Greg did?" Robin suddenly remembered her encounter with Greg in the lane when she had told him about Ted Coombes and the red hatband. It seemed like a lifetime ago.

He had been at Anna's funeral, of course. His grief

at losing her was obvious to see. Robin had wound her arms around him then, her mum had kissed him, and her dad had patted his shoulder, trying to let him know that they acknowledged his loss as well as their own.

She had only glimpsed him at a distance since then. He wasn't one to show his feelings. Robin felt she would have liked to have got to know him better, but now… She dragged her thoughts back to the present.

"I told him I thought the cow-cutter could be Ted Coombes. He was the one in Mr Tarrant's field that day, remember? He has a red hatband. Did he find out it was him?"

"You won't believe this, then. Greg went and had a row with Coombes, quite a noisy one, apparently. But there was nothing to point directly to him as the culprit – he's not the only one with a red hatband – so Greg had to leave off.

"He had been the one in Tarrant's field, of course, probably drunk as a lord. You know what he's like when he's full of cider. He just wanted to lather up those pretty little Channel Island cows and put them off their milk. He would consider that sport, especially if he annoyed Mr Tarrant.

"Ted is a sly one – and a stirrer. He loves nothing better than scandal and mystery. But *he's* got to be the one who solves it all. He just loves being one up on people. So…" Steff paused, relishing what he was going to say.

"Don't stop now!" Robin poked him once more.

"Well, he made it his business to discover who the cow-cutter really was. Greg said Ted Coombes patrolled fields and lurked about with cattle at all hours, until he had the culprit in his sights. Then he jumped him, gave him a beating, and dragged the man all the way to Greg's farm – the front door, mark you, and presented him."

"I don't believe it!"

"Straight up. Greg said he was such a weedy specimen of a man, and Ted Coombes had roughed him up so well, he almost felt sorry for him. Came from Porlock way, probably a bit touched."

Robin smiled wryly. "So Greg didn't get to kill him, then."

"He just rang for the police. I'd like to've been there to see it."

"Mmmm."

Robin was glad that it was Ted Coombes and not Greg who had beaten up the cow-cutter. Greg had been made to feel stupid by the dreadful Coombes, true, but his cattle were safe and if he hadn't accused Coombes that day, it wouldn't have been cleared up so fast. Funny to think she and Steff had set that ball rolling; it seemed ages ago when they were up by the quarry.

Robin grappled with her memories as she thought: one thing is certain, there has been quite enough violence in Godmore.

Silence descended again.

Robin roused herself.

"I'm off to London next week," she told Steff finally. "It's better if I go, and I want to. Mum and Dad agree. I'll stay with Mum's cousin and apply for art school. Give you a break from the rescue business." She tried to say it with a smile, but her mouth went crooked. She was going to miss him badly.

"I'll see August through here," Steff said. "After all this, I need to be alone for a bit. Then I'll sell the van and go home."

"Home?"

"Yeah. University calls. This was my year out." He smiled a little sheepishly at her. "I live in London too."

"You fraud!" Robin punched him. "I thought you were some sort of nature poet!"

"Oh, but I am…" Steff protested lightly. "Only … even in paradise one has to face reality."

"Reality." Robin's hand sought the silver locket lying under her shirt.

She would always wear it. The aching gap that Anna's death had left in her heart could never be filled, but slowly, she was beginning to be aware of another feeling. A sense of … being Robin only, and not always one of two. Anna would always be part of her being, that went without saying. It was like breathing in and out. When, at last, this terrible grief began to fade, knowing that fact would begin to be a comfort. But for now she had to get by as best she could.

It was like, Robin felt, she had been given permission to be separate. She wasn't sure that she wanted this gift, or what to do with it, but Anna had given it to her.

Steff turned to her suddenly.

"Tell me where you're living when you get to London, Roberta Robson. I'd like to know."

"Goes for you as well, Steffan," she answered him, gladness in her eyes and realizing that she didn't even know his other name.

Endings have beginnings too, she thought.